CHRISTMAS
COMES ONCE MORE

CHRISTMAS

COMES ONCE MORE

Stories and Poems
for the Holiday Season
Selected by MILDRED C. LUCKHARDT
and illustrated by
GRISHA DOTZENKO

Nashville   ABINGDON PRESS   *New York*

Appreciation is expressed to the following for their permission to use copyrighted material:

Augsburg Publishing House for Marjorie W. Brachlow's "Candles of Christmas" from their *1960 Christmas Annual.* Reprinted by permission of Augsburg Publishing House.

The Bobbs-Merrill Company, Inc., for "In the Great Walled Country" from *Why the Chimes Rang and Other Stories* by Raymond Macdonald Alden, copyright © 1906 by The Bobbs-Merrill Company, Inc., 1934 by Barbara Hitt Alden, used by special permission of the publishers. The Bobbs-Merrill Company, Inc.; and "The Boy Who Found the King" from *The Boy Who Found the King* by Raymond Macdonald Alden, copyright © 1922 by The Bobbs-Merrill Company, Inc., 1949 by Barbara Hitt Alden, used by special permission of the publishers, The Bobbs-Merrill Company, Inc.

Doubleday & Co., Inc., for "The Yule Tomte" from *Children of the Soil* by Nora Burglon. Copyright 1931, 1932 by Nora Burglon. Reprinted by permission of Doubleday & Co., Inc.

Friendship Press, Inc., for Elizabeth Whitehouse's "A Gift Should Be Given" from *More Missionary Stories to Tell*, Nina Millen, editor; and Elizabeth Allstrom's "The Lights of Christmas" from *The Round Window.*

Alice H. Gregg for "The Creche."

The Horn Book, Inc., for "Blessing of the Kindling," "Hospitality," "Wayfarers' Carol." Houghton Mifflin Company for an adaptation from Elizabeth Duryea's *The Long Christmas Eve*, copyright © 1954. Reprinted by permission of and arrangement with Houghton Mifflin Company, the authorized publishers.

J. B. Lippincott Company for a portion of Eleanor Farjeon's poem "Now Every Child" from *Poems for Children* by Eleanor Farjeon. Copyright 1927-1955 by Eleanor Farjeon. Published by J. B. Lippincott Company.

Charlotte Lohse for "Christmas in Summer."

The Macmillan Company for "For Christmas," by Rachel Field, from *Poems.* Copyright 1930 by The Macmillan Company, and used with their permission; "Nanka and Marianka Make the Big Christmas Bread" and "Old Grampa Makes Beautiful Things Out of Wood" from *Maminka's Children* by Elizabeth Orton Jones. Copyright 1940 by The Macmillan Company, and used with their permission.

Madeleine A. Miller for the poem "How Far to Bethlehem."

Harold Ober Associates, Incorporated for Eleanor Farjeon's "Now Every Child" from *Eleanor Farjeon's Poems for Children*, copyright © 1927 by Eleanor Farjeon. Reprinted by permission of Harold Ober Associates, Incorporated.

G. P. Putnam's Sons for "At Old Trinity," from Anne Carroll Moore's *Nicholas*, copyright 1924, (R) 1952 by Anne Carroll Moore. Reprinted by permission of G. P. Putnam's Sons.

Charles Scribner's Sons for Katherine Milhous's "Christmas Eve in the Wilderness." Reprinted with the permission of Charles Scribner's Sons from *Snow Over Bethlehem*, pages 18-26, by Katherine Milhous. Copyright 1945, Katherine Milhous.

Story Parade, Inc., for "Christmas Is Remembering" by Elsie Binns; copyright 1945 by *Story Parade, Inc.* Reprinted by permission.

Trails for Juniors, Board of Education, The Methodist Church and N. Carr Grace, executrix for Frances Frost estate, for the poem "Tree of Birds" by Frances Frost.

UNICEF for "The Creche" by Elizabeth Coatsworth from *The Children Came Running.*

United Press International for Louis Cassels' "Tribal Thoughts for Christmas."

The Viking Press, Inc., for "Now Christmas Comes" from *Miss Hickory* by Carolyn Sherwin Bailey. Copyright 1946 by Carolyn Sherwin Bailey. Reprinted by permission of The Viking Press, Inc.; and "The Day-Star" from *Dobry* by Monica Shannon. Used by permission of The Viking Press, Inc.

Whittlesey House, a division of McGraw-Hill Book Co., Inc., for "Christmas in the Valley," an adaptation from *The Beatinest Boy* by Jesse Stuart. Copyright © 1953 by Jesse Stuart.

THIS BOOK IS DEDICATED TO THE MEMORY OF

ANNE CARROLL MOORE

DOCTOR OF HUMANE LETTERS

WHO THOROUGHLY ENJOYED THE ENTIRE CHRISTMAS SEASON
FROM THE BEGINNING OF ADVENT THROUGH TWELFTH NIGHT,
AND WHO, THE WHOLE YEAR 'ROUND,
THROUGH HER PERSONALITY AND BY WAY OF BOOKS,
LIGHTED THE ROADS OF CHILDHOOD
WITH A WONDERFUL VISION OF DISCOVERY AND ADVENTURE,
OF HAPPINESS AND WORLD-WIDE FRIENDLINESS.

Special appreciation is expressed to Marcia Dalphin for her advice and encouragement in selecting stories and poems for this collection, and for her continual, unselfish guidance in the field of children's books.

Mildred C. Luckhardt

Foreword

To wish you joy as Christmas comes once more!

CHRISTMAS IS COMING. Boys and girls tell this delightful news in many different languages, in many different countries. While they make ready for the wonderful day, they decorate their homes and fill the air with the music of Christmas carols. We, too, sing with the world-wide chorus, "Let every heart prepare him room."

One beautiful way to prepare hearts for the coming of the Christ child is with the shining candles of an Advent Wreath. This lovely custom comes from Europe and has spread around the world. Perhaps you will make an Advent Wreath this year, and you may choose to tell some stories from this book when you light the candles.

Four weeks before Christmas, on the first Sunday of Advent, the first candle on the wreath is lighted in joyful expectation of the coming of Jesus. Someone then tells a Christmas story or poem. According to an old German custom, a paper star is added to the wreath each Sunday, with an Old Testament verse on one side and a New Testament verse on the other. These are to be memorized and thought about during the week. The Advent candle is kept burning during the time of wonder and worship, and before the light is blown out, carols are sung together.

On the second Sunday of Advent, the first candle is again lighted, and then the second. While both candles shine, Christmas stories, verses, carols, and prayers are once more shared. Each successive Sunday in Advent, one more candle shines in the wreath.

On Christmas Eve, after the four Advent candles are lighted, a special birthday candle is added for Jesus, the Light of the World. Then, in the mysterious beauty of Christmas Eve candle-light, the Christmas story is read from the Gospels and carols are sung to welcome the baby Jesus into the heart.

Merry Christmas to you all, this year and every year!

MILDRED C. LUCKHARDT

Contents

CONTENTS

CHRISTMAS COMES ONCE MORE

Christmas Comes Once More

Where Charity stands watching
And Faith holds wide the door,
The dark night wakes, the glory breaks,
And Christmas comes once more.

PHILLIPS BROOKS
(*from "O Little Town of Bethlehem"*)

At Old Trinity

EVERY YEAR, *as Christmas drew nigh, Anne Carroll Moore traveled with delight the starlit road to Bethlehem to stand in wonder before the Child in the manger. In her book* Nicholas, *she told of going to Bethlehem one Christmas Eve in a very old New York church with many people from many different countries, all singing together.*

TRINITY CHURCH was full of children when Nicholas came in with his new friends.

"We are just in time," whispered Ann Caraway as they slipped into the only vacant seat near the mysterious doorway.

As Nicholas turned to look again at the closed doors he saw above them, all along the organ loft, not one, but many flags—the flags of other countries. "I like to see the flags here," he whispered to Ann Caraway. Then, as he sat quite still, smelling the fragrant pine and watching the candles burn above the roses on the altar—far, far away he heard boys' voices singing:

> It came upon the midnight clear
> That glorious song of old.

A door to the left of the chancel opened and out streamed the choir. All over the church the children rose up, looking as if they were starting on a wonderful journey. Down one side aisle came the choir and up another, circling the church, still singing:

14

Look now, for glad and golden hours
Come swiftly on the wing.

The Bishop and clergy walked at the end of the procession and then they all took their places in the chancel.

Very clearly and beautifully the Bishop told the story of the first Christmas Eve and invited everybody sitting there in Trinity Church to go on a pilgrimage to Bethlehem. The mysterious doors then opened, and deep in the old doorway stood a manger with the figures of the Christ Child and the Virgin Mary, the Shepherds with their sheep, and the Wise Men with their gifts.

At the call of trumpets the choir boys rose, and led by trumpeters, they came down the central aisle to the mysterious doorway singing, "Noel, Noel." Behind the choir came the clergy and the Bishop, then came the children—hundreds of children from all over the city—

and the mothers and fathers and friends who had come with them walked beside them.

Everyone paused before the manger, then up the right-hand aisle moved the long procession singing, "Good King Wenceslas." Through mysterious rooms behind the altar the children followed choir and clergy singing one old carol after another. Down the left-hand aisle they came until at last everyone had passed by the manger.

As Nicholas and Ann Caraway slipped back into their seats the choir boys were singing:

O, little town of Bethlehem.

Later, as they turned to go out from the church by the side door they met the Bishop wishing everybody a happy Christmas and looking as if the wish had already come true for himself.

When Ann Caraway spoke to him, he said, "I look forward to this Christmas Eve visit to Bethlehem all through the year, quite as eagerly as the children do."

"That must be why it seems so real," thought Nicholas.

ANNE CARROLL MOORE

Tribal Thoughts for Christmas

Whoever on the night of the
Celebration of the birth of Christ
Carries warm water and a sleeping mat
    for a weary stranger,
Gives wood from his own fire
To a helpless neighbor,
Takes medicine to one sick with malaria,

Brings words of peace
To one who is bound with fear,
Gives food to children
Who are thin and hungry,

Provides a torch for a traveler
In the forest,
Sings a new song
For the young people
Dancing under the stars,

Visits a timid friend
Who would like to know about Christ,

Whoever does these things
Will receive gifts of happiness

He will have peace,
As one whose rice harvest is great,
And who hears his neighbors
Praise the exploits of his youth.
So will you receive happiness
If you do these acts of love and service
On the night of the celebration of Christmas,
The birth of Christ.

Loma Tribal Chant

How Far to Bethlehem?

It isn't far to Bethlehem Town!
It's anywhere that Christ comes down
And finds in people's friendly face
A welcome and abiding place.
The road to Bethlehem runs right through
The homes of folks like me and you.

MADELEINE S. MILLER

Christmas Eve in the Wilderness

FOR A VERY LONG TIME *people have been going to Bethlehem for Christmas. They have gone by train, by auto, by stagecoach, in ox-cart, on packhorse, on foot—but never on camel's back. For this is Bethlehem, U.S.A. Here the snow-covered hills of Pennsylvania replace the sun-baked plains of Judea, the fir tree replaces the palm. And at the Christmas season a great star, the evening star, hangs over the town—but it shines in the west, not the east.*

All through the country at Christmas there are thousands of towns and cities as brilliantly lighted—or almost. But there is something deep and deeply moving about Bethlehem that is nowhere else to be found. Here is the old Moravian church with its high, domed

19

belfry. To this church children go eagerly on Christmas Eve for the Children's Love Feast. Here they sing some of the glorious Christmas hymns which their ancestors brought from Moravia and Bohemia more than two hundred years ago. In the homes of this "Christmas City" families and their visitors kneel before the mangers, or putzes, which they have been making beautiful for weeks, to honor the birthday of the Christ Child. And a Christmas welcome reaches out to all who come to the manger.

Long ago, in the year 1741, before the place even had a name, the first settlers kept Christmas in a lonely snow-bound log cabin. Their special friend and protector, Count von Zinzendorf, had ridden through the snow-covered wilderness to celebrate Christmas with them.

As they were singing their old-world hymns, they heard the lowing of the cattle in the adjoining room—for their home, their chapel, and their stable were all under one roof. Following their leader into the the stable, they joined with him in singing:

> *"Not Jerusalem,*
> *No, from Bethlehem*
> *We receive life and salvation."*

On that Christmas Eve, that place received its name. In the delightful book, Snow Over Bethlehem, *by Katherine Milhous, Sister Gertrand tells the tale to the school children.*

"Once upon a time, on the shortest day of the year, the Count, our great leader, came riding out of the east. Beside him rode his daughter Benigna, a beautiful young girl of sixteen. They were accompanied by three young men on packhorses and the packhorses were loaded down with heavy sacks. The party had been traveling for days up hill and down dale. At last they reached the Blue Mountains, which, as you know, are not very far from here. Deep snow lay on the ground.

"Benigna was tired and a bit frightened as her horse kept slipping on the hard snow crust. It was Christmastime, and she missed her home in the old world city. She missed the tall church spires and the bells that chimed out above the holiday crowds.

"Now the party was riding over the brow of a hill. All was white and empty as far as Benigna could see. Was it for this, this white emptiness, that her father had left his duchy and all his loved ones, except herself? Her father, who was Count and Lord of Zinzendorf, and Berthelsdorf, and Pottendorf?

" 'Father,' she cried, 'there are no houses in this new land.'

" 'None but the wigwams of the Indians, my daughter.'

"They rode on. Benigna thought of the red men she had met from time to time along the way. She had tried to talk to them, but the Indians had not understood her, nor she them.

" 'Father, there are no church spires in this strange country.'

" 'Those are the only spires, my child,' said the Count, pointing to the pines and hemlocks that towered above the other trees.

"Dusk was gathering. Benigna shivered. When she spoke again, her voice had a sob in it. 'Father,' she cried, 'Father, there are no people anywhere.'

" 'There are our Brethren,' the Count answered. 'See, daughter, over there, where the evening star shines? If we follow the star, God willing, we will reach our Brethren tonight.'

"So they followed the star. As it grew darker, the sky became more and more full of stars. They snapped and sparkled over the world below. By their light Benigna could see that the valley was round and white like a porringer of milk. Down into this white valley they rode and kept on until they came to a creek. The young men lighted flares and the horses forded the creek, and they rode on. All at once Benigna cried out.

"'Father! I see lights through the trees.'

"'There, daughter, is our house, and our church, and our people —all under one roof.'

"They made their way through the trees and soon came to a clearing. In the middle of the clearing stood a long log house. Snow had drifted high against the sides of the house. It had piled up on the roof and was hanging down over the eaves, almost hiding the windows. Lights gleamed from the peepholes of windows at one end of the house. The other end was quite dark.

"Benigna waited while her father dismounted. She watched him walk across the clearing and knock at the door of the house. The door opened and she saw the people embrace her father and heard them cry, 'Brother Ludwig! Welcome, Brother Ludwig!' Now two boys came out of the house and ran toward her. One held a lantern while the other helped her alight from her horse. The three young men put out their flares and accompanied her into the house. The long journey was over.

"The two boys, James and Benjamin, stayed to look after the horses. Benjamin took the sack from the packhorses and dragged them across the snow into the stable which was in the unlighted part of the house. For, you see, the people and their cattle lived under the same roof. There was only a log wall between them. James led the travelers' horses into the stalls. Now, what with the cows and oxen already in the stable, every stall was full. This pleased James very much, for he loved animals. Benjamin stood by holding the lantern until all the horses had been fed and watered. Then the two boys went through a door in the log partition into their own living room.

"About the roaring fire the visitors sat warming themselves and eating little cakes of corn meal and honey that the women had quickly baked in the oven. They washed down the cakes with a drink of roasted rye. Benigna looked so beautiful in the firelight that James and Benjamin fell completely in love with her, and heard scarcely a word of the wonderful stories the Count was telling of his travels.

"Early the next morning James went into the stable. He curried all the horses well, but the coat of Benigna's horse he rubbed until it shone like a new chestnut.

"The next day, which was the day before Christmas, Benjamin went hunting and fishing. He was a lazy lout, but this he would do for love of Benigna. Such a grand young lady, he thought, could not be expected to live on corncakes and rye the rest of her life.

"While Benjamin was out hunting, James cleaned the stable. This he did for love of the animals, but especially for love of Benigna's horse, for so grand a horse ought not to stay in a filthy stable on Christmas Eve, the night on which the cattle were said to speak to each other in human speech. James put fresh straw in all the stalls and afterward swept the dirty rubbish over the doorsill and sent it flying across the hard snow crust. When he went to put back the broom in a dark corner of the stable, he noticed the three large sacks that had been taken from the visitors' packhorses on the night of their arrival. He thought it would do no harm to take just a peep. When he saw what the sacks contained, he grabbed the broom again and danced with it round and round on the barn floor.

"Suddenly he stood still and stared out the open doorway. The whole length of the path from the doorsill to where the pile of rubbish lay was black with birds. They were pecking at the grains of fodder that had dropped when he had carried out the old straw.

Around the pile of rubbish was a circle of rabbits and squirrels, nibbling and gnawing. Standing knee-deep in the hay was a young fawn.

"James hurled the broom across the floor. The noise it made when it fell startled the birds so that they fluttered up in the air, the rabbits scurried into the brush, and the squirrels ran up the trees. But the young fawn scarcely raised its head, so hungry it was. Even when James came up the path it did not run away, but stood and looked at him with mournful dark eyes. James put his arm around the fawn's neck, and led it into the stable. He made a bed of fresh straw in a corner for the little deer to lie on and gave it new milk to drink. It had just finished when Benjamin came back from hunting, empty-handed. Although he had tramped for miles and miles through the woods and fields, he had had no luck.

"When he saw the fawn in the stable, he was very much surprised. James saw him staring at it and guessed what was in his mind. He took Benjamin by the arm and said, 'Come, look! I will show you something better than venison for our Christmas dinner.' He opened one of the sacks just a crack, and Benjamin was so pleased at what he saw that he went over and hugged the fawn. He promised not to tell anyone about it, for fear that James would not be allowed to keep it.

"By now it had grown dark. It was Christmas Eve and the people in the next room were preparing to celebrate the birth of the Christ Child. The room was green with pine and hemlock and fragrant with their odor. Benigna went about with lighted taper and, as she walked, candle after candle leaped into flame. As James and Benjamin came into the room, the women were laying the cloth for supper. The people in the house had not much more to eat than the deer and the rabbits in the forests and fields. It had been a hard winter for man and beast. But the people were grateful to be warm and safe, free to make their home and found their church in this new land. And, added to all that, they had our beloved leader to rejoice with them on this Christmas Eve.

"Just as they were about to sit down to their poor little supper, the three young men slipped away and disappeared into the stable. They soon came back dragging three sacks, the contents of which they began to unload upon the table. Out of the sacks came all kinds of smoked meats, coffee beans, and fresh eggs, marzipan cookies and bottles of wine.

" 'These are gifts greater than gold, frankincense and myrrh,' said the people as they feasted their eyes, while the women prepared the real feast to come. And now Benjamin was very glad that he had not killed a deer to get venison for the Christmas meal. A little later, as everyone sat about the table talking and eating, visitors knocked at the door. Word had gone about the countryside that the Count and his party had arrived, and throughout the evening men and women from all the settlements around came to see him. Even the friendly Indians came.

"They came also because it was Christmas Eve, and Christmas has always been our great day. As the night wore on and talk quieted down, it was in the hearts of all of them to thank God for His goodness to them. Since they had no other chapel except this room in which they were sitting, our leader simply stood up and began a hymn, one which he had written himself. Soon all were singing, even the Indians. Benigna, the boys thought, sang like an angel.

"Hymn followed hymn, and the sound of the singing swelled and rolled like organ music in a cathedral. Every now and then, as the melody ebbed, there came the lowing of the cattle in the next room.

All at once the Count took up a candle, and, still singing, walked slowly into the stable. The people followed and stood about the cleared space on the floor. They saw the cattle blinking in the light, but the fawn trembling in his corner they never noticed, because James and Benjamin went and stood in front of its bed.

"Now the Count began to lead in singing one of our hymns, written long ago in the old world. It is one you all know; the one which begins:

> Not Jerusalem
> But Bethlehem.

"As the people sang, they began to understand. Here was the stable such as the one in which the Christ Child had been born. Here were the cattle who heard His first cry. Here were they, the people, who had come to worship Him. And all about in the deep forests were the savage Indians, and in the new cities men full of understanding. Gradually the singing died down. When the leader spoke, he put into words the thought that was in the hearts of all of them:

" 'Let this place be called Bethlehem.'

"It was Benigna who first noticed the young fawn on his bed of straw. Tugging at the Count's sleeve, she pulled him over to the dark corner. Then she smiled and whispered: "But father, there were no deer in the stable of Bethlehem of Judea."

" 'But in the new world Bethlehem,' answered her father, 'there must always be deer.'

"So James kept the fawn, and after a while, Benjamin came to love it almost as much as James did. If the animals spoke that Christmas midnight, you may be sure they had plenty to say to each other, especially the young fawn.

"And from that night on the place was called Bethlehem. Around the first log house a fine big town has now grown. Every year many people come to the chapel in Bethlehem to hear the story I have just told you. It is our Christmas story."

KATHERINE MILHOUS

Child Jesus

When the Christ-Child to this world came down,
He left for us His throne and crown,
He lay in a manger, all pure and fair,
Of straw and hay His bed so bare.
But high in heaven the star shone bright,
And the oxen watched by the Babe that night.
    Hallelujah! Child Jesus!

Oh, come, ye sinful and ye who mourn,
Forgetting all your sin and sadness,
In the city of David a Child is born,
Who doth bring us heav'nly gladness.
Then let us to the manger go,
To see the Christ who hath loved us so.
    Hallelujah! Christ Jesus!

HANS CHRISTIAN ANDERSEN

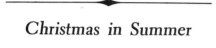

Christmas in Summer

It was Sale Day in the first week of December when I heard about the Christmas party. That was the day Dad sold Betsy, the roan mare. I'll always remember it because I loved Betsy and I was feeling pretty low. I was eleven and a half, and the last two years I had been helping Dad drive the stock into Mooltana, a handful of a place in the far northern end of South Australia. It had been fun that morning, riding the mare through our township. It was a clear hot day. The sun glittered on the glossy young steers as they jostled each other along the narrow street, kicking up great clouds of dust and filling the quiet little town with noisy bawling.

The townspeople kept their children off the streets on Sale Day. They were afraid of the long-horned flighty steers. But I rode right behind them, cracking my long whip and keeping them in order. Now and then Betsy reared up on her hind legs, and it was all exciting and sort of glorious.

But when I got in the hooded buggy to drive home with Mum, who had come in to do some shopping, it seemed all the good had gone out of the day. It was going to be awfully lonely without the roan mare. Mum gave me her special slow smile, but I knew she wasn't feeling happy either. You see I just rode Betsy to keep her in shape for Mum, because the roan really belonged to her. Sometimes I thought Mum cared more for Betsy than she did for Dad and me together.

Times were skimpy, and there'd been talking of selling Betsy for quite a while. The night before I'd heard Dad talking to Mum.

"If Old Man Riley offers a topnotch price perhaps we should sell."

Mum's voice was quiet. "Of course, Tim," she said to Dad. "I know Betsy is a luxury we can't afford these days. There are so many other things we need."

I fell asleep in my little room next to the kitchen thinking hopefully that Mr. Riley was a hard bargain-maker and that perhaps he wouldn't even be at the sale. He was, though, and he must have really wanted the mare because he paid a whopping good price for her. In spite of the money, I saw Dad's face when it happened, and it was as long as mine. I knew Dad would never have sold Betsy if there had been any other way.

Now I glanced up at Mum as she drove the gray ponies through the town. She was looking straight ahead, and I had the odd feeling that she was far away even though she was sitting right next to me.

When we came to the big brown house at the end of the street, Mum pulled up the grays. Doctor Brenner's house that was. "Little Doctor" we called him, and we loved him and brought him things from the farm whenever we came into town.

"Hop into the house," Mum said. "It's too late to visit. Give the doctor our regards and tell him we'll see him next Sale Day."

From under the buggy seat she got out a basket carefully covered with a big white tea towel and handed it to me. Eggs, clotted cream, cake, and homemade sausages were inside. I'd helped Mum pack them early that morning.

I pulled out the shiny brass knob on the front door and let it spring back, listening to the harsh clangy sound it made echoing down the long passage. Little Doctor himself opened the door.

"Why, Timmie Holden," he said, "I haven't seen you for months. Where's the rest of your family? Aren't you coming in?"

I explained that we couldn't visit because Mum had a sick calf at home and we'd stayed too long at the sale already. And that Dad had had to stay in town.

"Well, anyway," he said, "I want to talk to your mother."

We went through the big front garden, out to the buggy. Little Doctor shook hands with Mum and asked about everyone in the family. Then he said, "Look here, Mrs. Holden, we've made plans for a Christmas party for the children. I've asked everyone in the town, but I'd like the farm people to come in, too."

Mum said, "A Christmas party! Why, Doctor, I haven't thought about celebrating Christmas for years. Not since I left England."

Little Doctor's blue eyes twinkled. "That's what I thought," he said. "It's high time the children around here saw a Christmas tree. And that's another thing, Mrs. Holden; the best pine trees grow on that hill back of your place. Do you suppose big Tim and young Timmie here could bring in a tree a few days before Christmas?"

Mum's cheeks got pink the way they do when she's all stirred up. "Oh, I'm sure they could. A tall tree with thick wide branches. How high . . . how high could it be?"

Little Doctor laughed. You could see that he was pleased that Mum was so excited. "Well," he said, "we're having the party in the Town Hall, so I think the tallest tree to be found would be all right." He mopped his face with a big handkerchief. "I hope the good Lord will send us a cool day for it," he said.

The grays were kicking up a fuss, anxious to be off. "I say," Little Doctor called after us as we started off, "don't forget to get the news around. I want everyone to come."

Mum had often told me about Christmas in England, but I wanted to get everything fresh in mind, so I had a million questions. Our farm is fifteen miles north of Mooltana, so we had a long drive ahead of us. It was near sundown, but even when the sun was gone it would still be hot. The thermometer hadn't been below 102 degrees for weeks.

"This time of the year in England," Mum said softly, "it's cold, biting clear cold. When we children came in from school our cheeks and ears were stinging with the lovely icy cold." She sighed. "I'd love to feel that way just once more."

"Funny," I said, "freezing cold there and boiling hot here." I thought how nice it would be to see the other side of the world where everything was different. "Let me drive, Mum," I said, "you just talk."

The last bit of sun had slipped behind the faraway Flinders Range. It would be dark soon, but I knew I didn't have to worry about the grays. They knew the way and when they're heading for home they trot along at a good spanking pace.

"Snow falling," Mum said. "Oh, Timmie, some day you must see the snow fall; you must feel the thick soft soundless flakes against your face, and watch them turn the world into a fairy tale."

It was black dark now, but soon the sky would be lit with stars. I like driving at night. The buggy wheels rolling and the clop-clop of the grays are part of the big quiet feeling that comes over me.

"A few days before Christmas," Mum went on, "a tall pine tree is set up inside the house, and all sorts of glittery pretty things hung on it with a golden angel on the topmost branch. All around the bottom of the tree presents are heaped, secret presents for everyone from everyone else."

For a while we stayed quiet. I thought about snow and Christmas trees and tidy small villages where people lived close to each other.

Mum, I suppose, was thinking about when she was a little girl. Suddenly I wondered if she wished she were back in England, and I didn't like that thought at all. Then I started thinking about secret presents. I tasted the words in my mouth. Maybe . . . maybe there was some way I could give Mum a secret present for Christmas. Perhaps I could get Betsy back!

At the gate of the home paddock I gave Mum the reins and jumped down to open the gate. She sighed when I got back in the buggy. "We should have kept up Christmas here," she said, "but it's always so hot, it just doesn't seem to belong."

That was Saturday, the third of December. Next day I had to ride over to the Rileys' for a special setting of eggs that Mrs. Riley had promised Mum. First off, of course, I told them about the party. Dora Riley, who is only seven, said, "What's a Christmas tree?" I started to tell her, then suddenly I remembered that I didn't really know. She hung around, her black curls bobbing, her blue eyes wide, while I packed the eggs into my saddle bag.

"Ask your Granny about Christmas," I said. "She ought to know."

I suppose it seems queer that none of us knew about Christmas trees, but in the far north of South Australia it's hot most of the year. December is summertime, and the twenty-fifth often enough is a fair scorcher. So our families, who are all hard-working farmers, never bothered to celebrate.

As I got ready to swing into the saddle and get started home, Mr. Riley came out of the harness room with a bridle through his arm. "Thought I'd try out the mare," he said. So I walked over to the stable paddock with him.

Sometimes Betsy made a fuss about being caught. I never had much trouble because I could sort of catch up with her, but Mr. Riley was heavy on his feet. Every time he got near the mare she frisked on her heels and got away. By the time he finally got the bridle on her, Mr. Riley was red and sweaty and his temper was short.

"Does she always act up that way?" he asked.

"Not always, Mr. Riley," I said.

Suddenly I felt a warm growing hope inside me. Mr. Riley was an all-right sort of person, and if I explained about a Christmas present for Mum, and if the mare kept on being troublesome . . . maybe Mr. Riley would sell her back to me.

You see, I had quite a bit of money of my own at home. My gran in England sent me a gold sovereign every birthday. Mum kept them in a little black tin box with a lock on it. When I was eight she gave me the key and told me the money was my responsibility. The shiny japanned box with gold lines painted round it was on my mind a lot, lying solidly underneath all the other things I thought about. I did whatever odd jobs I could to make more, and in the September Michaelmas Holidays I'd added quite a little to Gran's money by helping Mr. Riley fix his boundary fences.

Ever since I can remember I'd decided what I would do with the money when I had saved enough. I wanted a black mare that was really my own. I wanted to ride through the hills when the golden wattle was in flower. I wanted to take the high jumps in the stable paddock the way Mum did. I dreamed of the day I would enter my own horse in the Mooltana Show and take a couple of prizes. There was about enough money now in the tin box to buy a good horse, but this new idea of a surprise present for Mum sort of shunted the little black horse out of my mind.

School is only six miles from our place, so on Monday I managed to get there before the Rileys and tell the news first about the Chrismas party. At playtime they all crowded around me.

"Yes," I said for the hundredth time, "everyone is invited. Little Doctor wants everyone to come."

Before Doctor Brenner settled in Mooltana, and that was only a few years ago, there wasn't a doctor within hundreds of miles. Most of the boys and girls had occasion to know him. He was what was called "square dinkum"—gentle and full of fun. You forgot to be scared even if a tooth had to be yanked out. So if Little Doctor was giving a party we all knew it would be something special.

Every playtime from that day was full of talk about it. The girls stood around under the big gum tree, whispering and giggling about what they were going to wear. We boys pitched horseshoes and took it in our stride.

Billie Riley said carelessly, "Be glad to help you chop down that pine for the Christmas tree. Pa said we could have the dray to take it in to Mooltana. Says he's got to see the Little Doctor anyhow."

Dad was extra busy. So Billie, Mr. Riley, and I walked over every bit of the pine hill looking for the best tree. We found a beauty. It had thick outspread branches with fat brown cones on them, and it was tall and strong. We sat down on some stumps and rested a while after we got it cut down. Now was my chance I thought. I watched Mr. Riley tamp down the tobacco in his pipe. After he got his smoke going I started to explain.

He listened quietly while I told him how badly Mum missed the roan mare, how she loved to ride.

"I know," he said, "Life here is kind of hard on your ma. Still and all, Timmie, I paid good money for the mare."

"I can give you a pound more than you paid for her," I said trying to keep my voice steady, "and . . . I want very much to give Betsy to Mum for a Christmas present."

He looked at me for a moment and my heart sank to my boots.

"My gran in England sends me money every birthday you know, and. . . ."

"Yes, I know," he said. "Want to spend it on your ma, eh, Tim? Well," he grinned, "I've been losing my temper regular with that mare. It's a bargain, Timmie."

We shook hands on it. "If we could get Betsy into Mooltana today," I said, "Little Doctor would keep her in his stables till the party."

Back at the farm while Mr. Riley was talking to Dad, I dashed up to my room and emptied the sovereigns into a little canvas bag, that usually carried my marbles, tying the open end with a piece of string. For a minute I felt a little sick inside. It would be a long time before I could think of owning a beautiful black horse and taking a prize at the show.

I rode Betsy into Mooltana from the Riley place, with Mr. Riley and Billie and the tree in the dray beside me. We stopped at the Little Doctor's house, and it was all right with him so I left Betsy in his stable the few days till Christmas. He got in the dray with us and helped get the tree into the Town Hall.

Billie's eyes popped at the piles of cardboard boxes stacked up at one end of the Hall. "What do you suppose?" he said in a loud whisper. But Little Doctor hurried us outside. "That's a fine tree you brought," he said. "I'm much obliged to you."

When I got home Mum had the bedroom all spread out with things from the old tin trunk, a small worried frown between her eyes. She was looking at some thin white stuff with pink rosebuds sprigged on it.

"This will make a lovely dress for little Dora Riley," she said, half to herself. That stuff had been a dress Mum had worn to the church social. I remember how pretty she'd looked. She was small as a minute and slim, and her eyes were deep, deep brown.

We were up before sunrise on the morning of the twenty-fourth. Like a miracle it rained during the night. It was fine helping Mum with the farm chores. The earth looked as though it had just been scrubbed, and the scent steaming up from it was a strange lovely mixture of all growing things. The woodbine creeper was still trembly with raindrops and sweeter than honey. I stuck my nose into the cabbage rose by the back gate, and the pink squashy petals were wet and spicy.

I was helping Mum with the milking when the sun came up. The old gray kookaburra in the gum tree began to chuckle, then worked himself up to rowdy laughter, the way he always does at sunrise. "It won't be dusty driving in, and it will be cool all day," said Dad, who, tired as he was, had started to get interested in the party along with Mum and me.

We climbed into the double-seater buggy a bit before one. We had to pick up some of the Rileys because they don't own a buggy big enough for all of them. It was half-past five before we got to Mooltana and six before we had the horses unharnessed, and ourselves tidied up. Mum had made over one of Dad's old suits for me, and pressed one of Dad's old ties for him so it looked like new. Her green dress looked pretty with a new frill. We all felt quite handsome.

The Town Hall is just a plain wooden building. It's like a barn inside with wooden rafters, kerosene lamps swinging from the ceiling on long chains, and a raised wooden stage at one end. But it didn't look like itself when we got there that evening. All the bare windows were garlanded with gumtree branches. Chinese lanterns, dozens of them, were strung across the room. There was an all-over sound of voices and laughter, not loud but excited and happy. Little Doctor and Mrs. Brenner were being everywhere at once. And in the center of the room was the tree!

So that was a Christmas tree! I wanted to sit by myself and really look at it. It reached almost to the ceiling, and hundreds of little white wax candles were perched on the branches. Packages in bright colored paper dangled, and heaps of them were piled around the bottom. The golden angel was there, too, just as Mum had told me, floating on the top branch as though she watched over the whole thing.

After Little Doctor was sure we were all there he got up on the stage and told us how he'd tried to make the tree like the one he'd had as a boy. "Only thing," he said, "I couldn't manage the snow for outdoors."

Well, then the presents were given out. They'd been ordered weeks before from Adelaide over three hundred miles away. There were presents for everyone and some left over. Tops, paint boxes, balls, books, cricket bats, pocket knives, dolls, sewing sets, doll furniture. . . . The sighs and o-ohs and a-ahs went around the room in waves.

Dora Riley came running over to me with a china doll. "Look, Timmie, she's got a petticoat, shoes, and a hat . . . and they all come off."

I got Kipling's *Jungle Book* (Little Doctor knew I was keen about Kipling) and a big bag of marbles.

After the presents were given out, Tim Mahoney, the constable, and Dad climbed on ladders and lit the little candles on the tree. "Looks as though the stars came down to roost, Timmie," Mum said. But I didn't want to talk.

Later Dad came over and sat beside us. "I've something special

for you, Timmie," he said, sort of awkwardly. I unwrapped the box he handed me, and inside was a heavy round glass ball with a green Christmas tree painted inside. When I turned it upside down the inside was filled with whirling tiny white blobs. "So you'll know about snow falling," Dad said.

It was beautiful. And to know Dad had had Dr. Brenner get it for him when he sent for the other presents! I turned it and turned it and thought I would never get tired of looking at it.

"Mum," I said looking up. But Mum's eyes were filled with tears. Suddenly I felt heavy inside me and I thought again, "Mum wants to live in England; she doesn't really like it here."

We had supper—sandwiches, milk, cocoa, cake, and little biscuits with "hundreds and thousands" sprinkled on top of them. We were the last to leave and Doctor Brenner who was at the door saying goodnight to everyone, walked with us to where Dad was harnessing the horses to the buggy in the Town Hall paddock. And there standing by the buggy was Betsy. Little Doctor put his arm around my shoulders. I was shaking with excitement. Then he shoved me forward gently. I went to the mare and handed the reins to Mum.

"It's my Christmas present, Mum, I said. "I bought her back for you."

"Betsy," Mum said softly, "darling Betsy." Then she turned to me. "But I don't understand, Timmie . . . it's not possible, how could you?" Then after a minute she said, "Oh, Timmie, Gran's money . . . you spent Gran's money for me. The money that was to buy the little black horse. Timmie, Timmie."

"Gosh, Mum," I said, feeling awkward and funny about it. "I'd rather have Betsy around anyway."

Then Dad was there and the slow look he gave me told me he was pleased with what I'd done. But Mum bent down and kissed me and her cheek was wet against mine. Billie Riley rode the mare to our farm and planned to spend the night with us. I sat on the back seat of the buggy with Mum, as Mr. Riley was up front with Dad. She tucked her arm around me.

"Such a lovely, lovely evening, wasn't it, Timmie?" Mum asked.

I leaned against her. "Mum," I said because I still wasn't sure, "if you could live anywhere you wanted, where would you choose?"

For a second there wasn't a sound. Then Mum started to laugh, a happy bubbling sound. "What a foolish, foolish question, Timmie love," she said. "Only one place of course, I chose it long ago; right here on the farm with you and your father . . . and Betsy. You've been worrying about those tears back at the party. They were happy ones. But, oh, Timmie, I did miss Betsy. It was silly of me, but you've made everything perfect." I could feel her looking at me seriously. "I love Australia, too, Timmie, even though I wasn't born here."

I cupped the glass between my hands and wished that particular moment would last forever. The Southern Cross sprawled big and brilliant against the sky. The buggy wheels, the trotting grays and Betsy's clip-clop behind us melted into nothingness.

Next thing I knew Mum was shaking me gently. "Wake up, Timmie dear," she said, "and help your father with the horses. We're home again, and it's Christmas Day."

CHARLOTTE LOHSE

The Creche

Come, hang the greens and plant the Tree
  And light the Christmas candles;
Your carols sing of Wise Men Three,—
  Or shepherds in their sandals.

Go build again the wooden bed,
  The cattle standing round it,
The straw to pillow His sweet head,
  The Shepherds to surround it.

Then kneel beside the manger bed,
  And feel the loving awe
That takes all simple-hearted folk
  Who kneel upon the straw.

ALICE H. GREGG

Old Grampa Makes Beautiful Things Out of Wood

"MAMINKA!" shouted Nanka, running down the stairs to the kitchen. "Four more days till Christmas!"

"Yes, my little mouse, I know," said Maminka. "Na, run along!"

"Aunt Pantsy!" shouted Nanka, running up the stairs again. "Four more days till—"

"Christmas!" said Aunt Pantsy, giving Nanka a hug. "Run along, my good girl!"

"Old Grampa!" shouted Nanka, running down the stairs again. She opened the door to his room. "Four more days—Yi! Is that your secret, Old Grampa?"

Old Grampa motioned her to come in, and to shut the door behind her. Nanka tiptoed around Old Grampa's bed to where he sat by the window, whittling with his sharp knife. Whittle-whittle-whittle! went Old Grampa's sharp knife. On Old Grampa's table stood a tiny stable, with a roof of straw.

"What is here?" asked Nanka. And Old Grampa answered, "Betlem." Then he held out two tiny persons for her to see.

She took one in each hand, very carefully. One was a man with a bald head and a beard. He had a long robe on. He was bending over. "What's his name?" asked Nanka.

"Josef," answered Old Grampa.

The other tiny person was a woman, with a halo on her head.

She was kneeling and reaching out her hands. "What's her name?" asked Nanka.

"Maria," answered Old Grampa.

Nanka put Josef and Maria, very carefully, inside the stable. Then she rested her chin on the edge of the table, and looked and looked and looked, because she loved the tiny Josef and the Maria that Old Grampa had made out of wood.

Next morning there were only three more days till Christmas.

"Old Grampa!" shouted Nanka, knocking at his door. "Three more days!" Then she opened the door and slipped inside.

There was no sound in Old Grampa's room but the whittle-whittle-whittle! of his sharp knife. He sat by the window, making three more tiny persons out of wood. When they were finished, he held them out for Nanka to see. They were kings, with fancy crowns on and long robes and cloaks on. Two had long beards, and one held a little round box. The long-bearded two were bending over, like Josef. The one with the box was kneeling, like Maria.

"Who are these?" asked Nanka.

"Kraly," answered Old Grampa.

Nanka put the Kraly, very carefully, beside the stable, where Josef and Maria were. Then she rested her chin on the edge of the table, and looked and looked and looked, because she loved the tiny Kraly that Old Grampa had made out of wood.

Next morning there were only two more days till Christmas.

"Old Grampa!" shouted Nanka, knocking at his door. "Two more days!" And she opened the door and slipped inside.

Old Grampa had already finished two more tiny persons, and he was whittling a third with his sharp knife. The two were angels with wings on. One of them, the smaller, was carrying flowers. The other was carrying fruit.

"What's her name?" asked Nanka, touching, very carefully, the wings of the one who was carrying fruit.

"Marianka," answered Old Grampa.

"What's *her* name?" asked Nanka, quickly pointing to the tinier wings of the one who was carrying flowers.

"Nanka," said Old Grampa quietly.

"Yi!" said Nanka not so quietly.

Then Old Grampa finished the other tiny person. It was a little boy, with a big hat on. He was kneeling, like Maria, and carrying fruit, like Marianka.

"Honzichek!" guessed Nanka right away. And Old Grampa nodded his head.

Nanka put the three, very carefully, beside the stable, where Josef and Maria and the Kraly were. Then she rested her chin on the edge of the table, and looked and looked and looked, because she loved the tiny Nanka, the Marianka, and the Honzichek that Old Grampa had made out of wood.

Next morning was the morning of Christmas Eve.

"Old Grampa!" shouted Nanka, opening his door. "Christmas Eve!" She ran to the table where the stable stood.

And there, at last, by Maria lay the tiniest Baby that Nanka had ever seen, on some hay, with a tiny wooden feather bed to cover Him. "Jezishek," Old Grampa explained.

Maria was reaching out her hands to the tiny Jezishek. Josef was bending over Him. The Kraly were bowing and kneeling. And Nanka, Marianka, and Honzichek were bringing flowers and fruit to him.

"You beautiful little Jezishek!" whispered Nanka.

Then she rested her chin on the edge of the table, and smiled and smiled and smiled. She loved the little Jezishek best of all. Old

Grampa nodded his head, and wrinkled up his face, as he put his sharp knife away. He loved the little Jezishek, too!

ELIZABETH ORTON JONES

Light Ye Up Your Candles

Then be ye glad, good people,
This night of all the year,
And light ye up your candles,
For His star it shineth clear.

Old English Carol

Candles of Christmas

Candles of Christmas! Deep in their warming light
Are shepherds' fires, a guiding star at night,
The holy radiance of a Baby's birth—
The Christ, who brought the light of God to earth.

MARJORIE W. BRACHLOW

The Advent Wreath

ON A PLEASANT SLOPE on a mountainside, there was a village called Friendly. Just Friendly—nothing less, nothing more! What more, thought its people, could anyone want than to live in this village? Old Bartel, the clockmaker, heartily agreed. When he was a lonely youth he had come here and found friendliness. Also, he had found here his rosy-cheeked bride, Netta. And year after year he and Netta lived happily in this village they loved, growing old among friendly neighbors.

One bright September afternoon, old Bartel and Netta and their granddaughter, Linya, bustled about their house, preparing to go next day down the mountain to sell Bartel's clocks at the Fair in the city. Linya was delighted to make the trip, but wished all her village playmates might go, too.

As she packed clothing near the window, she could see children running back and forth across the road to each other's houses. A singing brook tumbled along down the west side of the road, and children clattered across the small footbridges that spanned it. By good luck the clockmaker's house stood on a sort of tiny island in the middle of the road. In front of the house the brook rippled in a wide swoop across the road, then almost circled the house and turned again, dancing downhill from the village along the east side of the road.

While Linya watched, children came running down the middle of the road and skipped across one of the footbridges that led into her house. Karl, a boy her age, came in first calling, Linya, here's a toy for you to play with while you're in the city. My father made it." He handed her a carved wooden goat, whose head bucked up and down when she pulled a string.

"Oh, thank you, Karl!" she cried. "And thank your father, too." She held it so all the children could see and admire. They agreed that Gard, Karl's father, certainly could make toys that were fun to play with.

Soon women neighbors came with baskets of bread and cheese, fragrant apples and nuts, delicious smelling plum cakes and ginger cakes, to tuck into Bartel's oxcart for him and Netta and Linya to eat when going to the Fair.

While Linya stood sniffing the tempting food, Netta thanked her neighbors. She laughed and exclaimed, "One would think we were going far away instead of to the foot of the mountain. Still, good food from good neighbors tastes just right any time, any place."

Just then a big man strode in, with a heavy oxbow on his shoulders. "Bartel," his voice boomed, "I have made you a new ox yoke for the trip. Tomorrow morning I shall come early and put it on your oxen."

"Oh, thank you, thank you, Rudi," replied Bartel. "You knew that the old yoke had a crack. How kind you are! How kind are all the people in our village!"

"It was not always so," said Karl's mother, the wife of Gard. Their house was at the end of the village just across the road from the home of Rudi and his family. She looked around the room to be sure that all the children were listening. "In days long, long ago, so the story goes, two unfriendly families lived in this village. One family, with its uncles, aunts, cousins, children, grandchildren, and other relatives, built houses along the west side of the road. The other had houses on the east side."

Another woman took up the tale, "They never crossed the road to share a tasty bit of food with each other, or sing together, or play games. In those days when our village was divided it had no name. It was a hateful place."

"Oh, but that was long ago and never could happen to us," cried Margaritte, Karl's lovely older sister. "How sad it would be if we each kept to our own side of the road because we did not like those opposite."

Then everybody laughed, and Margaritte blushed. For she was betrothed to marry Rudi's oldest son, the young man across the road. They would wed when he returned with the other lads bringing home the flocks from the summer pastures higher in the mountains.

As they laughed together, a merry chorus of cuckoo clocks sang, "Cuckoo, cuckoo, cuckoo"; and Linya exclaimed, "Even the cuckoos mock us when we talk about unfriendly times in our village."

Next morning right after breakfast, the whole village turned out to help the clockmaker load his cart for the Fair. Very carefully, Gard and Rudi, the two biggest men in the village, carried gay little cuckoo clocks to the cart, while each one in the village found a job to do to help. They promised to feed the bird, the cat and the dog, and the goat while Bartel's family were gone.

When Linya, at last, climbed into the cart beside her grandparents, it slowly started off. Neighbors ran alongside for a way calling, "May you have a good trip." "We will be waiting when you return next week."

They were, indeed, waiting when the clockmaker's family returned. But there were no cheery greetings, no laughter. At sight of the oxcart, two separate groups of people ran toward Bartel shouting in horrid clamor, "mean," "stupid." Each group herded together on opposite sides of the road.

Linya was frightened. Netta cried, "What is this? What have we done?"

Bartel was a patient man, and kind; but if need be he could be stern. So, although amazed by what went on, he stood up in the cart, clapped his hands and shouted "Silence!" Everyone was dumbstruck. Nobody knew Bartel could be so commanding.

His voice was clear and steady. "This is a harsh welcome. Let one person explain."

Immediately two towering men began talking in big, roaring voices. One was Rudi from the west side; the other was Gard, from the east side. As they tried to outshout each other, all Bartel or his family could make out was "Troublemaker! Robber! Lies!"

This time Bartel stepped from the cart and walked slowly, calmly, toward the big, shouting men. Standing before them he looked up into their angry faces, placed his hands over his ears, shut his eyes and mouth tight. They stopped short, staring down at him. Then he said quietly, "I will not listen to men roaring like wild animals. If you have a complaint, speak in turn—Gard first for half a minute, then Rudi."

Gard's words tumbled out so fast that neither Bartel, nor Netta, nor Linya caught them all, but they did get some idea of what had happened. During a high windstorm, a branch of a pine tree from behind Rudi's house blew across the road at the very moment that Gard's wife came out of their door with a bucket of yellow paint. The branch struck the paint bucket, splashing yellow paint all over Gard's wife. The next-door neighbor told Gard that Rudi's wife laughed and said Gard's wife looked like a withered yellow squash.

Rudi broke in, "Everyone knows what a bad temper Gard's wife has. She threw the paint kettle across the road and splattered paint all over my wife's sheets that were drying."

Gard cried, "Rudi took the pine branch and scratched our door."

Rudi shouted, "Gard threw it across the road and broke the roses in our garden."

"Then Rudi threw it back across the road and it landed in front of our house," Gard declared angrily. "He refuses to move it, and I will not carry away his trash."

Rudi's face puffed up with rage. He shouted, "We will not clean the road for the east side. Let them stay on their own side."

"And you stay on your side," screamed Gard's wife.

When it seemed that everyone would burst out quarreling again, Bartel silenced them. "Go to your homes. Get back to work, and as you work pray that our heavenly Father will take the anger from your hearts."

Bartel, too, went to his work and prayers. But he was constantly interrupted during the next days by persons from each side, coming to tell him of new wrongs done by the other side. Linya trembled at sight of these angry neighbors. West side came by the west door, and stormed out when east side came in. East side did the same. No matter how Bartel pleaded, the feud grew.

Linya was very unhappy. The autumn would soon turn into winter; and before long all the village should begin planning for Christmas. But how could angry people share Jesus' birthday?

"Perhaps," she thought, "when the young men bring the goats and cows down from summer pastures, all will be well. That is such a happy day. Then we will all go to the wedding of Margaritte and Paul; and Rudi and Gard and their families will make friends again. Then our village will be friendly once more."

The whole household arose early on the day the flocks came home. From high along the mountain path could be heard the young men singing and calling as they returned after the long summer. "Surely," said Bartel to Linya, "as they all come singing home together, nobody will divide them."

However, doors were flung open on each side of the road, and west side stamped together up the path, while east side did the same on the other side. Only Gard's daughter, Margaritte, stayed indoors.

"Poor Margaritte!" Netta sighed. "No doubt her father forbade her to go to meet Rudi's son."

The singing on the mountain path suddenly stopped. Soon, two solemn processions of animals and young men came into the village on opposite sides of the road, following their families. Rudi's son, Paul, looked toward Margaritte's house, but his father quickly turned him to the west.

Linya could hardly bear to go to school those days, for children from the west sat with the west, and east with east, as their parents had ordered. She spoke with them all, as she always had done, but times had changed. Those who had been good friends came to distrust each other. The schoolmaster tried to reason with them, then punish. It was all no use.

"It is as if kindness and friendliness were dead in our village," Linya sighed to herself as she went home from school. "What sort of a Christmas will this be? I only wish there was some way we could bring about peace again. Oh! I wish for a miracle!"

In the little chapel, the pastor tried to guide his people toward peace. He went from house to house in the cold November evenings, trying to persuade them. But their hearts were hard. Even when he became ill from cold and weariness, they did not seem to care.

However, each day Netta cooked him warm meals and Bartel and Linya took turns carrying the food to his house. Once Linya met Margaritte there, sweeping the floor, while Paul brought in wood and built up the pastor's fire. Whenever Linya went the house was clean and the fire warm and crackling. But she told nobody except her grandparents. Then, one day, Bartel took the sick man to stay with cousins in another village, but good pastor promised to be back by Christmas.

Every Saturday Linya went with Netta and Bartel to sweep and dust the church as they had done with the rest of the village for years. It was a lonely job, and hard work, for just the three of them. Perhaps, the next day, though, the villagers would come to church once more to worship, even though the pastor was still too ill to preach. But each Sunday, only the clockmaker's family worshiped in the village church.

"Hatred drive people away from God and from each other!" Netta whispered as they climbed the lonely hill to church on the last Sunday in November.

Linya blinked back tears. "Will nobody bring green branches into church and decorate it for Christmas with stars and bells and candles? Will nobody come here to sing Christmas carols while you play the violin, Grandfather?" She began to cry.

"Little one," replied her grandfather, "let us go into church and pray for a miracle of Christmas peace for our village."

As they entered, they saw Paul and Margaritte and her younger brother Karl reverently kneeling in the front of the church. Linya knelt beside her grandparents and prayed. Outside all was still, not as before when neighbors came up the road singing and talking, glad to go to church together. Now there was no Sunday singing, in church or out, no happy laughter, no friendly Sunday dinners together.

But Bartel was smiling when they left the church. "Hurry!" he urged. "While I prayed I received an idea straight from heaven. While we eat dinner, I will tell you."

So Linya and Netta flew around getting dinner, while Bartel gathered armfuls of fragrant evergreen from trees near the door, whistling all the while. However, he would say nothing about his heaven-sent idea until they sat down to eat by the cozy hearth.

"Netta, if you are willing, we shall invite all the village to our house tonight."

Linya gasped. "All the village together! Fighting?"

"When I invite them, they must promise to be polite," answered Bartel. "Do you and Grandmother have enough cookies baked so we can share a little treat with them?"

They nodded. So he explained, "This is the first Sunday in Advent season. Linya, do you understand what that means?"

"I understand," Linya exclaimed. "During Advent we make ready for Christmas. We make our houses clean and beautiful and decorate the church. We make gifts, and sing carols, and prepare a feast."

Grandfather agreed. "However, while we make our homes ready, we must make our hearts ready, also, to receive Jesus. When I was a boy, people in our city made Advent wreaths to prepare our hearts for him. Come! We will make one, too."

He stretched his arms in a wide circle. "We will make it this large, for it will be a wreath for a whole village. We will place it on our table." He started shifting their big table toward the center of the room, and Netta and Linya helped.

"I don't understand how a big wreath, no matter how beautiful, will help our neighbors make their hearts ready for Jesus," said Linya.

Grandfather pulled one of her braids. "We shall hope for a Christmas miracle in their hearts. Now, run out and get some pretty pine cones."

Linya still did not understand. She gathered the cones from the frosty ground quickly and hurried indoors again. Grandfather explained only a bit at a time, while they all worked at making the wreath. They had twined Christmas wreaths for their home before, but this was the largest they ever had made.

When it was nearly finished, Grandfather moved his work-worn hand slowly over it, saying "This beautiful circle of fresh evergreen is a symbol that God is everlasting."

He told Linya to bring four green candles, and he showed her how to stand each one upright in the wreath.

"These candles are symbols of the light that is come into the world with Jesus," he explained. "Each Sunday evening during Advent we light another candle and prepare our hearts for him."

"Now," said Grandfather, "bring a white candle." She selected one that was tall and perfect. "This, said he, "will be the special birthday candle which we light on Christmas Eve for Jesus, the Light of the World." He stood it firmly in the wreath.

Linya decorated the wreath with pine cones. and thought of the Christmas miracle that Grandfather had prayed for. Oh, if only kindness and peace would come alive in their village again! She hoped Grandfather would not be disappointed. Yet she feared he was expecting too much.

While she and Grandmother set out cookies and prepared hot chocolate to reheat later, Grandfather went to invite their guests. He stood briefly at each door, smiled, and gave his message. Then he crossed the road and did the same at another house. Light snow was falling, and his footsteps showed, back and forth across the road— the only footsteps that had crossed and recrossed in many weeks. Linya was proud of him as he walked bravely from Rudi's door to Gard's. Would his plan work? Could there possibly be a miracle?

Soon, rosy-cheeked with the cold, he clumped across their east-side footbridge and into their warm home. "Everyone will come, and bring his own cup for chocolate. I told west to sit on the west side of the room, and east on east, and asked them to be polite because they are guests. They will come when the first star is seen."

Warming his hands by the fire, he said, "Now, we shall make our own star. Linya, please bring a sheet of the white paper that we bought at the Fair."

With swift, sure lines, he drew a five-pointed star while Linya wondered what would be next. "Now," he said, "on each side of this star we write a message from the Bible. We shall add another star and another Bible verse each week in Advent."

As Netta cut out the star, Linya and Grandfather turned pages in the big family Bible until they found suitable selections from the prophet Isaiah. As Linya carefully wrote them on the star, Grandfather explained, "When I give the signal tonight, Linya, please read these verses and light the first Advent candle."

She felt proud, and scared, too. She kept repeating the verses while helping get supper, because she wanted to read them without mistake. She was still repeating them when she watched out of the window for the first star of evening. As soon as it shone people came from their homes silently down each side of the snowy road.

By separate doors they entered the clockmaker's house; and by the cheering firelight found places in the shadowy room. Many sat on the floor. They were careful to sit on their own sides. Rudi's son, Paul, and Gard's daughter, Margaritte, sat nearest to each other—although on opposite sides of the hearth.

Bartel told everyone about the Advent wreath and its meaning. He read from the Bible, "Prepare your hearts unto the Lord." Then he turned its pages and read "The spirit of man is the candle of the Lord."

Next he looked all around the room and said, "We will now light the candles for Christmas. Listen carefully to what is said, for I hope that each evening during the coming week when you light the lights in your homes, every family will repeat the verses from Holy Scripture which we hear tonight."

With trembling hands, Linya carried a lighted taper from the fireplace to the Advent wreath on the table in the center of the big room. As she lighted the first candle, people whispered, admiring the beautiful wreath. She held the paper star and read by candlelight, "For unto us a child is born, . . . and his name shall be called . . . The Prince of Peace."

There was not a sound in the room when she turned the star and read, "How beautiful upon the mountains are the feet of him that bringeth good tidings, that publisheth peace." During the hush that followed, Bartel bowed his head and prayed, "Our Father, as we light the candles of Christmas, may their glow shine in our hearts and lives."

When he stood up, he smiled at all the guests. Then Netta brought forward platters heaped high with cookies and placed them on the big table near the wreath. Margaritte and Paul sprang up to help her pour hot chocolate. Soon the room was filled with the buzz of persons sharing a treat. But, even though there was more happiness in that room than she had felt in the village for weeks, Linya was disappointed that nobody except her family and Margaritte and Paul went from one side to the other.

Later, when the guests left by separate doors, Grandfather invited them to come the next Sunday for the lighting of the second Advent candle.

In the morning, Linya hurried to school, hoping the miracle had happened. But the children still sat separated. All week no neighbors crossed the road to borrow raisins or spice for Christmas baking, nor to take samples of goodies to share. Perhaps, when the second Advent candle was lighted, their hearts would soften. Each week, when they came, Linya lit another candle and read more verses about the coming of Jesus. But she was discouraged, and sad for Grandfather, too.

He assured her, "We must not give up, but do our best with

God's help." Now came the fourth Sunday of Advent, and the villagers arrived. When they were seated, Linya moved to the fireplace to light her taper. Somehow, Paul and Margaritte each lighted a taper, also, and walked with her toward the Advent wreath. Together they lighted four candles, while all the neighbors watched. Margaritte and Paul's voices joined Linya's as she read, "The people that walked in darkness have seen a great light."

Together they turned the star. Then, sweetly, unexpectedly, came music from Grandfather's violin. Everyone turned quickly toward him and listened as he played the tune of the angel song that they always sang at the church door each Christmas. Slowly, one after another, on both sides of the room, people rose and began to sing, the same words that were written on the star:

Glory to God in the highest,
and on earth peace, good will toward men.

While they sang a second time, Margaritte walked gently among them, drawing together in the center of the room some from each side, who usually sang in the church choir. And when they finished that beautiful song, Bartel's violin led them in an old mountain carol, "Come to our hearts, O Prince of Peace." Now they needed no urging. Linya was overjoyed. She could see by their faces that a Christmas miracle was taking place. They were truly welcoming Jesus into their hearts.

When the music stopped, a lovely silence filled the room as neighbors looked across at each other, smiling. It was Rudi who clumped from his side across the imaginary barrier they had made. He strode up to Gard, and, partly to cover his feelings, boomed, "Do you and I go tomorrow as we always have done and gather evergreen branches to decorate the church?"

Gard's voice was loud, too, but a pleasant noise, as he bellowed back, "Everyone who wants to help Rudi and me, be ready right after breakfast."

"We'll help," came calls from all over the room, while people gathered together planning for the Christmas service as they had done for years.

Above the hum of voices, came the merry jingle of a bell. People stopped talking and looked around. Margaritte held high a little silver bell that had been on Netta's cupboard. Her eyes were shining as she cried, "Let us take the Advent Wreath to hang in the church for Christmas Eve. There, together, we may light the birthday candle."

So it came about in the little village of Friendly that each year families gather evergreens and twine Advent wreaths and light Advent candles to welcome Jesus. And every Christmas Eve they go singing to the church and light the birthday candle of the Prince of Peace.

MILDRED C. LUCKHARDT

Christmas Is Remembering

Christmas is remembering
Shy shepherds on a hill
And voices echoing
   "Peace—Good Will!"

Christmas is remembering
A stable and a star
And wise men journeying
   From afar.

Christmas is remembering
A new-born boy
And all the world caroling
   Songs of joy.

ELSIE BINNS

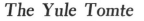

The Yule Tomte

GULDKLUMPEN tugged his weather-beaten sled up from the seashore. The big, empty sea chest on it was very heavy. Slipping, sliding, he pulled with all his strength until as far as the south wall of the goat house.

"What better place than this could a tomte want for himself?" thought Guldklumpen as he rested and admired the big chest he had found on the shore. Ever since his sister Nicolina told him that a tomte was the kind little elf man who brought good fortune to a home, he had been wishing a tomte would come to live with them.

Perhaps, if a tomte saw this house and liked it, good fortune would come to their little farm. They might even have some chickens who would provide them with eggs to eat, as was the case with the Liljecranz children. They had plenty of everything, and Nicolina said it was because a tomte lived with them.

Would it not be wonderful if the tomte made things easier for Mother, so she did not have to work so very hard to earn what she could with spinning and weaving and with making cheese from the milk of their little brown goat?

Guldklumpen hurried into the forest and lugged back spruce boughs. These he stuck in the ground about the house, to make a little forest for the tomte. Then he filled the house with sweet-smelling hay so the tomte would have a comfortable bed.

Still, there was something missing. The house must have a name. Otherwise, how would the tomte know it was meant for him? Guldklumpen found a piece of birch bark on the ground. He would need help printing the name, for he was not old enough to read and write well. He did not want to ask Mother. He wanted her to be surprised when the tomte took care of them; and to be the happiest mother in all Sweden's Norrland.

So he went and found his sister Nicolina knitting a red stocking by the fireplace. He whispered, "Nicolina, do you know how to spell tomte?"

Of course, she wanted to know why; and he whispered the whole secret right in her ear. So, after "TOMTE" was neatly printed on the bark, they tiptoed out and tacked it over the door of the little house. Nicolina told her brother, "The tomte would not like you to run out here, all the time, for it would seem the house did not belong to him."

Guldklumpen tried hard to keep away from the little house. He hoped the tomte would bring eggs for them to eat for Easter breakfast, as in bigger farms where people were richer. But he and Nicolina could keep away no longer, and crept down and peered in. In the hay was a whole nestful of eggs! Twelve eggs for Easter morning! Even rich people could not have more eggs on a day such as this!

Nicolina gathered them carefully in her apron and carried them home while Guldklumpen raced ahead with the news, "Mother, there is a tomte on our farm now!"

It was good to know a tomte was there, even though he brought them no more such surprises. Nevertheless, Nicolina and Guldklumpen kept hoping he might do some things that tomtes did on other farms. Meanwhile, month after month, they worked to earn money to someday buy a cow. Scarcely did they get home from school each day than they were out, combing the woodlands for juicy red lingon berries to sell at market.

One chilly afternoon, returning from market swinging their empty baskets, they realized the berry season was over. They could earn no more money that way for a while. "Probably we can buy the cow year after next if we save money and work hard," said Nicolina.

That was so far away, Guldklumpen could hardly think of it. The frosty road was cold and hard under his bare feet. Mother would want him to wear shoes now. His old shoes were worn out; the tomte had brought him no new ones; and Mother had no money to buy them. Nicolina said he might wear her old outgrown shoes. She had been given a larger pair outgrown by one of the Liljecranz girls.

"Me wear girl's shoes?" cried Guldklumpen. He certainly would not!"

However, next morning his mother said, "Wear Nicolina's shoes. They are almost new." When he started to scream and cry, the mother said it would be as she said. So he went to school wearing girl's shoes.

As soon as Guldklumpen reached school, Lars Ole's son, that whiney Aspen, saw he had been crying. Then Aspen saw the shoes! He called, "Look at mamma's little Guldklumpen wearing girls' shoes! Why aren't you wearing a hair ribbon, too?"

"Guldklumpen is a gir-l!" cried many voices.

Guldklumpen hurried toward the schoolhouse where he might be alone. Nicolina heard them and left her playmate. "Aspen," she said, "he is my brother, leave him be!"

Aspen called out, "It is because your mother is so poor she can't afford to buy you any shoes!" As he mocked Guldklumpen, he tried to knock off Nicolina's shawl.

Guldklumpen knew that because his mother paid all her debts she had no money. He flew at Aspen like a mad hornet, and pummeled him even though Aspen was much bigger.

"Teacher! Teacher!" Aspen ran screaming to tell the teacher that Guldklumpen hit him.

"Why did you hit Aspen?" the teacher asked. Guldklumpen would not tell that it was because Aspen said mean words about his mother. So the teacher said, "Guldklumpen, stand in the corner for the rest of the day!"

Nicolina's heart ached. Aspen came to his seat triumphant. "I knew he would catch it!" he whispered to Nicolina. She swung around and smacked him. Then Aspen cried out loudly that Nicolina hit him. Prayers were about to begin, so the teacher grabbed Aspen by the collar and sat him in a corner, too!

Guldklumpen did not hold a grudge against Aspen, however. He did not even tell his mother what had happened. Instead, he and Nicolina helped her get ready for winter. They gathered flax from the field, pounded it free from woody stems, then brought it inside in a tall basket to stand by the fire. There he helped comb the fibers and prepare them so his mother could spin. He filled the woodshed with wood, and kept the fire going.

One evening as they worked by the fire, they talked about Christmas. Mother told a story about the Christmas tomte who gave away all he had but one crust of bread, which he gave to a hungry sparrow on Christmas morning.

Guldklumpen could feel tears running down his cheeks, he was so sorry for the poor, kindhearted tomte. So his mother said, "Now I shall tell you a merry tale." And she told about the wonderful Yule tomte who brought Christmas gifts, and about his workshop and all his little helpers. She also told of the delicious Christmas pudding waiting for the tomte on Christmas morning after he returned home from his long journey about Scandinavia.

When the tale was over, Guldklumpen danced before the fire because the tomte got something that Yule. Then at bedtime, he asked wistfully, "Do you think we will get anything from the Yule tomte this year?"

His mother answered, "This year I am sure it is your turn." This made them so happy they wanted to talk about it half the night. The tomte had not come to them many times before. How wonderful, if he really would give them a gift this year, as he did to most of the children at school!

Next day at school the children told Christmas stories. Then during recess they all hurried across the road to see some new little piglets at the Widow Olsen's farm. "You needn't come!" said Aspen to Guldklumpen, and threw a stick at him.

Aspen ran ahead to catch up with the other children. Some already had climbed on the fence and were looking down at the great mother pig and her babies. She grunted shrilly and moved about the little white and pink bundles nervously. She did not like children, and tossed back her ears sending a warning snort to them.

Aspen pushed the smaller children off the fence to make room for himself. Guldklumpen came up now, on a pair of stilts the Liljecranz boy had left behind. On the stilts, Guldklumpen looked right over the others' heads. Aspen was boasting to the children how brave he was; and tried to push Nicolina off the fence. He lost his balance, and fell right into the pig pen! The mother pig ran at him, squealing with rage. The children fled for the school yard, leaving Aspen screaming. Guldklumpen scrambled up the fence carrying one stilt. He knocked the old pig as hard as he could. She let go of Aspen and sprang at Guldklumpen. He struck again with the stilt, and cried, "Hurry, Aspen!"

Aspen caught at the fence, but could find no foothold. Guldklumpen kept beating off the raging pig. He almost lost his balance as the stilt was jerked from him. But, somehow, he managed to grasp Aspen and together they fell over and down to the ground in safety.

Before long the whole school was cheering Guldklumpen. He smiled, shook his head and took out his reading book.

The next days were too full of work in school and at home to look backward. But Nicolina and Guldklumpen still wondered if the Yule tomte would give them anything.

Then came the very important day in school, when children would receive presents from the tomte. Nicolina was eager to go because there had been some talk of the Yule tomte's bringing apples. Guldklumpen doubted. How could the Yule tomte bring apples for all the children today when some winters he was so poor he had not so much as one apple to give to Guldklumpen and his sister!

In school when it was time for the gifts which lay under the tree to be passed out, Guldklumpen slumped down in his seat to make himself as small as possible. Sometimes children brought small gifts for each other; but no one ever gave Nicolina and Guldklumpen anything, for they had nothing to give in return.

Now the teacher was commencing to pass out the gifts! Nicolina turned and looked at her brother. She did not smile. Perhaps she, too, was wishing they hadn't come. Last year she had cried on her way home.

But the Yule tomte did bring the children apples! Nicolina and Guldklumpen were given the very finest. Guldklumpen hugged his. It was as large as half a pumpkin—almost and it smelled sweet! He was so happy he could hardly keep from talking out loud!

Suddenly, a big box was put down right on Guldklumpen's desk. "This is a mistake!" he gasped. "Probably it belongs to Lisa Liljecranz. I never get this much from the Yule tomte—not even at home."

But the schoolmaster asked, "Can anyone think why Guldklumpen should be given such a big gift by the Yule tomte this Christmas?"

Many hands went up, but Aspen did not know. Lisa Liljecranz said, "It is because Guldklumpen was brave and pulled Aspen out of the pig pen before he was badly hurt. My mother said it would not have been too much if Aspen had given Guldklumpen a Yule gift." Aspen didn't seem to hear. He was stuffing himself with sweetmeats.

Guldklumpen could not speak and say that he never had thought of being repaid for helping Aspen. He just sat looking at the wonderful box. It had a big, red ribbon made out of silk. He turned the box round and round. On one side was a picture of a Yule tomte, on the other an angel, and forests on both the other sides.

When the schoolmaster asked if he were not going to open the box, Guldklumpen replied, "I am going to take it home and let Mother untie the pretty bow!" The children coaxed him to open it but he shook his head. He did not want to lose what was in the box if he fell into a snowdrift.

He ran almost all the way home and fell twice, but got there before Nicolina. The door flew open and slammed closed again as he sprang into the cottage. He plunked the box down in his mother's lap. "I got it from the Yule tomte because I hauled Aspen out of the pig pen!"

"The Yule tomte!" echoed his mother. "Are you sure?"

"The teacher said so."

Guldklumpen urged her to open it. Just then Nicolina arrived carrying both the wonderful apples and came over to see what the box contained. The first thing was the card, which said it was from the tomte to Guldklumpen. One could see it had helped to build that tomte house this past spring, for last Christmas the tomte had not given them even a card!

The box was full of bags and parcels, packed close together. First there was a roll of coffee bread with sugar and cinnamon on top! Then sweetmeats, nuts, fruits! Guldklumpen laughed out loud for joy, and Nicolina was so surprised she stood and gasped, as more and more delicious things were unpacked.

"May we have some of the good things to eat?" cried Guldklumpen. Mother put the kettle on and made ready for their little feast. She had to smell the rosy apples and hear what happened at school. That evening as they sat at the table eating, they laughed and had a jolly time.

Then they took their sweet-smelling apples to bed and fell asleep with the fruit in their arms. That day would not soon be forgotten!

NORA BURGLON (*adapted*)

Blessing of the Kindling

I will kindle my fire this morning
In the presence of the holy angels of heaven,
In the presence of Ariel of the loveliest form,
In the presence of Uriel of the myriad charms,
Without malice, without jealousy, without envy,
Without fear, without terror of anyone under the sun,
But the Holy Son of God to shield me.

.　　.　　.　　.　　.　　.　　.　　.　　.　　.

God, kindle Thou in my heart within
A flame of love to my neighbour,
To my foe, to my friend, to my kindred all,
To the brave, to the knave, to the thrall,
O Son of the loveliest Mary,
From the lowliest thing that liveth,
To the name that is highest of all.

Celtic Rune

The Boy Who Found the King

THERE WAS ONCE a little kingdom in a pleasant valley, whose people thought themselves among the happiest in the world. Only one thing kept them unsatisfied. They had lost their King. At the center of their capital city was a beautiful palace with a presence chamber and a splendid throne, cared for by many servants and guarded by loyal courtiers and soldiers; but for years no one had lived in it, no one had sat on the throne, nor had it been used on feast days.

Once each year on Christmas Eve, the palace was brilliantly lighted and opened for all the citizens, according to an old custom of the kingdom. Then the throne was decked out for the festival, the ministers of state stood about it as if a king were there to whom they might do honor, and the people hoped each year that he would actually return in time for the Christmas celebration.

It was now many years since he had gone away. He was a young man then, but would now be so much older that some who had known him best were not certain whether they would recognize him when he came home. His people were still puzzled to understand why he had gone away. He had everything, it seemed, that a king could wish for, but had not been content to stay in his palace.

"I do not know how to be a good king," he said, "until I have seen other people than those of my own land, and have learned how to be of use as other people learn to be useful. So I shall leave my throne and become a pilgrim, and when I come back perhaps I shall deserve to be king."

For a time this was all very well. The ministers of state carried on the government in the King's absence, and no wars or other troubles made the people suffer, but they had always been loyal and devoted to their reigning sovereigns, and could not be happy while the palace and the throne were vacant.

So, after years had begun to pass, they sent messengers to various countries where they thought the king might have gone, asking the rulers of those countries to urge him to come home. But the rulers always replied that they had not seen him. It was supposed that he was still in the disguise of a pilgrim, and would not make himself known.

There had been some who thought that the King had not left his own land, or that he had returned to it and was living among his people without their knowledge, watching those who were managing the state so as to give them their just rewards and punishments.

At any rate, many citizens made a point of watching for the King, hoping to be able to recognize him in disguise; for they supposed that if anyone should discover him, and go boldly to him, saying "You are the King!" he would not deny it, but would yield to his people's wish and return to the throne. So now and again one would actually think he had made the discovery, would approach some stranger in the capital, saying "You are the King!" and would be sadly disappointed to find him shaking his head in surprise.

Once a man who had been so addressed actually said it was true —he was the king—and allowed himself to be led to the palace. But it was soon known that he was a pretender. Whether the ministers of state were able to recognize the King's face or not, they had a sure method of proving whether any stranger was really he.

The royal crown lay hidden in the treasure-chamber close to the throne, and no one but the King knew how to open the chamber. Some said that there was a single marvelous key which he had carried away with him, and others believed that the door of the treasure-chamber had a magical lock, of which only the King knew the secret, as it had been handed down by the kings that went before him.

So when the false claimant came into the palace, they received him courteously and led him to the throne-room; then he was requested to open the treasure-chamber. At first he pretended that he did not wish the crown—that he would wait until some greater occasion. But when the ministers insisted, he at last broke down and had to confess that he knew no more than they about the ancient lock.

Now there was a boy who lived in the capital city, an orphan, named Andrea. When he was still very young he began to wish for the King's return, having heard much talk of the matter from his father and mother before their death. His mother before her marriage had been a servant in the royal palace; and she had a treasure which few people in the kingdom possessed, a portrait of the young Prince—who was now the King. It was a beautiful picture, and showed a noble face with eyes so fine and friendly that Andrea was certain he would know them if he saw them anywhere. So it seemed to him that it might be both his duty and his good fortune to find the King.

Whatever spare time he could obtain, he would spend so far as possible in the places frequented by strangers, and would scan the faces of any whom he met. He used to lie awake in bed thinking of the ways in which he might make the discovery, or dreaming of the gratitude which the whole country would feel for the one who should accomplish what they all wished for; and he was resolved, when he was old enough to be his own master, to devote his whole time to the search.

When he was about twelve years old this opportunity came. His guardian's wife died, and the man himself was now so old and busy and sad that he gave little thought to the boy Andrea, who had always been so good as to require little watching. Now that the season came when he was not in school, Andrea was left quite to himself from morning till night. It became his habit to take his lunch with him, leaving the house early in the morning, and to spend the day in one or another part of the city—sometimes, too, going far into the surrounding country—where he thought there might be a chance of discovering the King.

He had begun this manner of life for only a few weeks, when there broke out a plague in the kingdom. It had been brought by pilgrims from the east, and soon spread rapidly from one village to another, then to the capital.

Presently a great hospital was established in a huge abandoned castle on the edge of the city where the sick were taken who had no one to care for them at home, and where many doctors and nurses worked night and day. It was sad to see the streets filled with wagons and litters carrying to the hospital those not able to walk. But neither Andrea nor any of his close friends had yet become sick.

One day, however, hearing men talk of the hospital, he said to himself, "Is not this the next place where I should go to look for the King? If he came to the city as a pilgrim, he would very possibly be taken with the plague and have to go there as a man without a home. Or, if he is as good a king as we all believe, he would at least visit the hospital to see if there was anything he could do for his suffering people. I must make some excuse to try to go inside and search. Think of the chance that the King should be lying sick and alone on a poor bed in that great lonely place!"

So next morning he went directly to the quarter of the city where the old castle stood. He could have found his way to it, even if he had not known, by the stream of litters and the hurrying doctors going and coming between its doors and the newer part of the city. Andrea found, however, that there was a guard at the entrance; any one who was neither doctor nor patient must show a pass.

So he went around the side of the building until he came to a small kitchen entrance in the wall at the lower end, where it approached the river; and here he waited to see what chance might bring. Presently an elderly porter came outside, carrying two great pails of refuse which he was to throw into the sewer-ditch that emptied into the river. Andrea offered his help with one of the pails, and when they were returning with them empty he asked if the porter would help him to go inside the hospital.

"Why do you wish to enter?" asked the porter. Andrea hesitated. "Have you friend inside?"

"It—may be," said Andrea.

"You have missed someone, perhaps, who you think may have been brought here?"

It was hard for Andrea to tell anything but the truth. "The real reason is," he said, blushing, "that I am looking for the King."

Andrea had expected the porter either to burst into a laugh at this, or to become very angry, but he did neither. Instead, he looked at the boy quietly and kindly, and asked, "Why do you suppose the King is among the patients here, or that you could discover if he were?"

Then Andrea gave him his reasons, and promised that if the porter would help him to an entrance, he would be exceedingly careful not to get in anyone's way or make any trouble. "But are you not afraid of catching the plague?" asked the porter.

"No," said Andrea. "I think I am too young and strong. But if I did, it would be quite worthwhile if only I could first find the King."

"Well," said the porter, at length, "I do not think I have the right to give you an entrance as a visitor, no matter what your purpose is. But if you should carry in one of the pails as my helper, and then take water for me up to the main floor where I am to do some cleaning you will probably find yourself where you wish to be."

Andrea thanked him warmly. "I shall be very glad to help you," he said. And presently he found himself in the servants' quarters in the basement, then on the narrow winding stairway that led to the main wards of the hospital.

He had scarcely reached the top of the stairs when a nurse, catching sight of him, said, "Boy, when you have taken that water where it is needed, do you not want to help me carry a sick man in to his bed? Everyone is so busy I have not been able to find a porter for the other end of the litter."

"Certainly," said Andrea.

When he had given the nurse the help asked for, he heard someone begging for a drink of water, and went to fetch it. Then he saw another patient shivering in a chill, and searched for a long time till he could bring a warmer blanket. From one moment to another it seemed that something was needed. Andrea was shocked at the suffering he saw in the hospital, and at the needs of poor stricken folk for whom there were far too few attendants.

It was well into the afternoon before he found a breathing space long enough to allow him to sit down and eat his lunch; and when that was over he began again to run errands for nurses, to answer the calls of sick men and women, or to help an occasional porter who was struggling with more than he could carry.

When it began to grow dark, Andrea made his way to the winding stair, that he might go out at the same gateway where he had entered; hoping, also, for a glimpse of the friendly porter who had let him in. He found him in the servants' quarters, looking very weary as he sat on a stool eating a bite of supper; and indeed Andrea's own legs were almost ready to give way under him.

"Well," said the porter, smiling at him, "have you had any success in your search?"

Andrea shook his head. "I have not even begun it," he said, "there has been so much to do. Until there is more help for the patients, I cannot think of the King at all."

The porter nodded. "It was just so with me," he said.

"Why," said Andrea, "you don't mean that you came also to look for the King? Are you not one of the regular servants here?"

"No, I did not come to find the King," he said, "but I came to look for a friend on the very day the hospital was opened; and I found so much to do that I have not been away for an hour since. There were more people willing to do nursing than to carry on the dirty work of porters, so I stayed downstairs to help with that."

"I am sure, then," said Andrea, "that you will let me in again tomorrow." And the porter promised that he would.

So it happened that, day after day, Andrea spent the hours of daylight in the great hospital, doing errands for doctors or nurses or patients. It was all so busy and so sad that he forgot all about the King.

One day a nurse—a kind woman with a motherly face—stopped as she passed Andrea in the corridor, and put her hand on his forehead. "Boy," she said, "your face is flushed, and I do not like the hot feel of your skin. You must go rest for a while at least, if you can find a bed to lie in."

Then Andrea realized that his head was aching badly. It had been aching most of the day, but he had been too busy to think of it. Meantime he finished the errand on which he had been sent; and by the time it was done he was almost too dizzy to stand. Should he try to go home, or ask for a patient's bed at the hospital? He stumbled down the winding stairway; and just as he reached the last step everything went black in his eyes, and he felt himself falling to the floor.

It was a long, long time before he knew anything more. If he had been aware of what was happening, he would have seen himself carried to one of the quietest corners in the hospital, put into a clean cot, and watched over by many of the attendants whom he had been helping during those busy days. As it was, days and nights went by like a long troubled dream, until, one morning, he seemed to know that the sun was shining into the window, a face was bending over him with a friendly smile, and a friendly voice speaking his name.

His eyes looked straight into the eyes that were smiling at him, and suddenly he knew them as if he had always known them, and he said, "You are the King!"

"Hush!" said the voice. "You must sleep now, and not talk."

"I have been sick?" said Andrea.

"Yes, a long time; but you are much better, and will be able to be out for Christmas." Then Andrea saw that the face and eyes had become those of his friend, the kind porter, and he was too tired to see or say anything more, but immediately fell asleep.

When he woke again, one of the nurses was sitting near him. "I am sure the plague must be much better," he said, "or you would have no time to sit down."

"Yes," she said, with a happy smile. "Yours was the last bad case, and now half our beds are empty."

"Was the porter from downstairs here," asked Andrea, "when I first woke up a while ago?"

"Yes. It was he that brought you up here, and he has spent every night by your bed since you were taken sick. Is he an old friend of yours?"

"Will you ask him to come in again," said Andrea, "as soon as you can?"

"Certainly," said the nurse; and she went to fetch him.

When the porter came near the bed, Andrea reached out his hand and took that of his friend. "Bend your head down," he said, "as you did before, so that I can see straight into your eyes. You ARE the King!"

The porter was silent for an instant. Then he said softly, "Yes, I am the King."

Andrea was too happy to speak for a little. "You said something about Christmas Day," he said at last. "Is it almost here?"

"Yes; in ten days."

"Then you will be at home for Christmas!"

When Christmas Eve came the air was fine and still and frosty, and the stars were very bright. As always, the great palace was beautifully illuminated, and the people of the city were making ready to go there for the festival. Yet some, especially the older courtiers and citizens, felt not a little sadness. Another year gone, and still no word or sign of the King. Perhaps he had died in the plague, and no one had known it.

The throne-room was crowded, and the lights were dazzling. From the royal chapel close by came the sound of boys chanting carols. There came up the entrance steps unnoticed by anyone among the multitudes, a tall stranger in a gray pilgrim's cloak, with a pale but happy-eyed boy at his side.

"Now," said the boy, "I will slip off into the crowd, and you must go forward where the Lord Chamberlain and the other officers are gathered about the throne."

"No," said the pilgrim, "I am too shy to go forward alone. It is you that brought me here, and you must take me all the way." He took the boy's hand in his, and they went forward to the brilliantly robed company of courtiers.

"Present me to the Lord Chamberlain," said the pilgrim.

The boy stepped forward boldly to where the Lord Chamberlain sat on a dais at the right of the throne, and said, in a clear voice, "If you please, my Lord Chamberlain, this is the King!"

The Lord Chamberlain looked down at the boy with an amused smile. "And who are you, sir?"

"It does not matter, sir; but my name is Andrea. I have found the King."

The Lord Chamberlain turned to the gray-cloaked pilgrim. "And is this your opinion, also, good stranger?"

"I have not denied what my friend the boy has said," was the stranger's reply.

The Lord Chamberlain's face wore a puzzled frown. He rose from his seat. "Then," he said, "will Your Majesty be so gracious as to open the treasure-chamber and release your crown?"

The pilgrim threw off his gray cloak and hood, and stood, a noble and commanding figure, though in plain dark clothing, in sight of all the courtiers. The guards made all who stood near leave a space, and opened a path to the treasure-chamber. As word sped about that something strange was happening, a silence fell on the company, and everyone stood motionless to watch.

The stranger advanced with great dignity to the door of the treasure-chamber, stopped there a moment, shutting his eyes as if to call up a long memory; then he stretched out his hand and touched lightly one of the carvings on the heavy bronze door. Instantly the door sprung open as if released by a secret spring. The lights of the audience-room were flashed back from the hundreds of jewels upon the royal crown that rested within. The King took it in both his hands, and turned back to his officers.

"It is not for the King," he said, "to crown himself."

The Lord Chamberlain and courtiers all bowed low as he passed them; the ushers led the way to the steps of the throne and prostrated themselves before it; while the oldest of the ministers of state, who had set the crown upon the King's head so many years before, stepped forward and took it from his royal master's hand. As he did so, he looked keenly into the King's eyes. "It is Your Majesty indeed," he said.

Then he set the crown upon his sovereign's head, and all the people cried, "Long live the King."

The boy Andrea had stepped back as far as possible; but the King, as soon as he was seated on the throne, beckoned to him and bade him stand close by his knee. Then, when the shouts were hushed the King spoke.

"My people," he said, "I have seemed to be a long time away, but I have known how it went with you, and it seemed to me that you scarcely needed a king. Only when the plague broke out, I started at once for my capital, and arrived as far as the door of the hospital. There I found I was needed much more than in the palace, and I remained there, serving the sick until today. But since my work there is done and you have wished for me to be here on my throne for the holiday festival, I have at last come openly to take my crown, and to wish you all from my heart a happy Christmas."

Then the people broke into shouting again, and tossed their caps and embraced one another, some laughing and some crying for joy, until the King put up his hand to command silence.

"I have one more thing to tell you," he said, "before we join in the procession to the cathedral for the service to welcome in Christmas Day. There were two reasons why I did not wish to come back sooner to the throne. One was that I had never yet found a way to serve my people, so as to feel that I deserved the crown. This recent time of suffering has given it to me. I did the hardest and least desired service I could find, and have borne your burdens with my own hands; so now I am a little more worthy to be king. The other reason was that I wished to find a successor; for you know it is the ancient law of our kingdom that, when the King has no children of his own, he shall name a prince to be trained as ruler in his place. It was in this time of trouble that I found him, and it seemed strange and beautiful to me that he alone, of all my people, recognized me, and was the one to bring me to you tonight. He has learned early what it took me a long time to find; he, too, has suffered with you, and borne your burdens; and I proclaim him Prince Royal on this happy night."

He drew Andrea close beside him, and took him by the hand. "Welcome the Prince Andrea," he said, "as you have welcomed me."

Then the shouts commenced again, but now it was "Long live the Prince!" "Hail Prince Andrea!" The boy himself was so dumb with astonishment that he could not have said a word to save his life.

Now there sounded the music for the great procession. The King and Andrea descended from the throne, and the ministers and courtiers led their way where the choir-boys were beginning the processional hymn to lead them to the cathedral. But before they reached the entrance, the royal attendants brought two shining robes of scarlet and cloth-of-gold, for the King and the Prince Royal to wear. And it happened, as they passed down the palace steps, that a poor old woman who had been one of the sick folk in the hospital, and to whom Andrea had brought water all through one night when she was parching with feverish thirst, was able to come close enough to reach the corner of his new princely garment and to press it to her lips.

RAYMOND MACDONALD ALDEN

What Can I Give Him?

What can I give Him,
   Poor as I am?
If I were a shepherd
   I would bring a lamb,
If I were a wise man
   I would do my part,—
Yet what I can I give Him—
   Give my heart.

CHRISTINA ROSSETTI

The Day-star

The Day-star of the Day-star
And we on earth who lay
In death-shade and in darkness
Have found a world of Light.
For, soothly, of a virgin
Is born the Lord of Light.

MONICA SHANNON

A Gift Should Be Given

HIGH UP ON the range of mountains that frowns upon the Black Sea, a tiny village clings to the rocky wall behind it. From the plain below, a winding road wanders into the foothills to lose itself finally among the trees. As the road climbs it becomes increasingly rough and narrow. At a certain point carriages and even horses must be left behind, and the traveler must proceed by foot. Beyond the village only the most experienced of guides can go. High above towers the huge granite pinnacle, which the plain dwellers said was inlaid with gold; they had watched it for centuries gleaming in the afternoon sun. No one in all the memory of the mountain village had ever climbed the smooth-sided pinnacle to claim its gold.

In the village dwelt the mountain guides and hunters, tall men with fearless eyes and strong, sure feet. Now and then a hunter wandered down to the plain below to sell his furs and his venison, but visitors came seldom to the village.

One day a hunter returned from the plain in great excitement: "I bring you news," he cried as he reached the first house. "Come to the church."

The hunter hurried through the village, and the long, crooked street was soon a hubbub of sound. Windows were thrown up and people shouted, "What's the news? What has happened?" But the hunter only called, "Come and hear," and pressed on to the very center of the village where stood the rough-hewn church. Doors opened and men, women, and children poured out, to follow the hurrying hunter.

As the people reached the little rustic church, the priest came forward to meet them.

"What is it, my son?" he asked as the hunter paused.

"I have heard, Father, that the prince of the land is coming to our village."

"Surely you have not heard aright," answered the little priest unbelievingly. "How should a great nobleman climb the mountain where not even the sturdiest of horses can make his way in safety?"

"They swear it is true," persisted the hunter. "Never before has such a thing happened, but it will soon be the birthday of the prince, and he wants to spend it among the humblest of all his father's people. He will make his way to us afoot, if need be."

The simple mountain folk were so surprised by the hunter's news that for a moment no one said a word. Then the priest spoke.

"We must make him welcome," he said. "Our village must look its best. Asaph, you must replace that stone from the roadway before your house. It has been missing for many a day, and we have stumbled as we passed. The road must be made smooth."

"I'll mend the broken hasp on my door," declared the oldest man in the village. "I had thought it did not matter. But it would be unsightly for the Great One to look upon."

"And I must look to my windows," declared the wife of the returning hunter. "They have not been cleaned for a long time. They must be clean and bright when the prince comes."

For days thereafter the villagers worked from morning to night. Mothers washed and mended and cleaned. Fathers and big brothers repaired their homes, which lined the one little street that composed the village. They smoothed and straightened out the road as best they could. They even climbed part way down the mountain to mark with fresh cuts the zigzag path by which the visiting prince must climb. At last everything seemed ready: only two days and the visitor would be among them.

"Is there nothing more we can do?" asked one.

"We might bring gifts to welcome him," suggested the man who lived in the biggest and snuggest house. The others were suddenly silent.

"We have no money to buy gifts, and nothing of worth of our own to give," they said at last, "nothing worthy of the Great One."

"He probably drinks from a cup of gold, and wears pearls for buttons on his commonest clothes," declared one. "What can we give to such as he?"

The little priest spoke then, "We can give him the most precious thing in all the world," he said. "We can give him our love. Some day he will be our ruler; he will command many, but may have few who will serve him with love. Then, perhaps, he will remember with joy the love we offered him. So take thought, offer the best you have with love, and your gift will be in all things perfect."

After that the villagers were very busy. The best cook in the village made loaves of fresh sweet bread for her gift, and love went in with the leaven. The trappers brought their choicest pelts and hung them in the church where the Great One would see them when he came. Some of the young wives brought bits of linen from their wedding chests. The young girls braided garlands of mountain flowers and trimmed the fronts of the houses where the Great One must pass. They filled the little church with flowers and with the sound of their happy laughter.

Only one little house was bare and quiet. Costah lived here with his little sister, Marja. Marja was too little to reach the rafters to hang the daisy garlands, and Costah was a guide and was gone all day, so there were no flowers on their home.

The night before the prince was to arrive, Costah talked long and solemnly to Marja. "Little sister," he said, "I have planned a beautiful gift for the Great One."

"What do you mean, brother?" asked Marja in surprise.

Costah turned a serious face to his sister. "I shall climb the pinnacle, and bring from there a slab of gold," he said.

"But, brother," cried Marja in fear, "no man has climbed the pinnacle. What if you should fall?"

"I shall not fall," answered Costah confidently. "While the others have worked in the village for the prince I have carried my ax and my hempen rope up the mountain, and there I have practiced what I must do. Trust me, little sister. The Great One shall see that I, too, can bring him a gift of love."

The next morning, bright and early, Costah started forth. "Goodby, little sister," he called. "Do not be frightened. You shall see how beautiful will be my gift for the prince. I shall lay it at the very foot of the altar."

That day the village was the most joyous in the whole world. The people could not pass in the street without stopping to greet each other with happy words, "Good day, neighbor, are you ready for the Great One?"

"Ready indeed! My house is clean, my gift is waiting and my heart is full of love," would be the joyous answer.

To Marja, however, the sunny hours of the morning were filled with fear for Costah and with sorrow for her own empty hands. At last she wrapped her ragged little shawl about her and started down the mountainside. She could not bear to join with the happy, waiting villagers. She would climb down the path, hiding behind the boulders, and watch for the Great One by herself.

"If I miss him," she said to herself, "I will listen for the church bell. It will ring when he arrives. I shall see him tomorrow. He will not expect a gift then."

Hours passed, but no climber approached the village. Marja's sharp eyes grew weary of watching. The red sun had slipped far down in the west when Marja decided to start back to the village. It was turning bitterly cold, and the little shawl was all too thin in which to brave the mountain chill when darkness came. Where was the Great One? Had the hunter's message been wrong, or had it been only a joke of the plainsfolk? How disappointed Costah would be!

Suddenly Marja stopped in the middle of the trail. She heard a groan. What was it? Approaching carefully she peeped around the side of a great rock and saw a man lying on his side on the moss. His face was white and drawn with pain, and his lips were blue with cold. His foot was crumpled up under him and the ankle was swollen terribly.

"Oh, you are hurt!" she cried pityingly.

"And cold," answered the traveler with a twisted smile. "I have lain here in the damp moss for hours. You see, I lost my way."

"I know that, sir," answered the child. "No one ever comes up here from the plains except . . ." She paused.

"Except what, my child?" said the stranger gently.

"Our prince was coming today," answered the child. "At least, we had thought so, but the villagers have waited all day for him. Now it is too late. Not even a Great One can find the trail in the dark. Oh, how cold you are!" She took the chilled hands of the traveler in both her own and warmed them. "Your coat is torn almost to shreds."

Half dragging him, she helped him to a dry stone where he might sit and lean against a gray boulder.

"Wait here," she said. "I will call the men. They will help you." Then drawing her thin shawl from her own shaking shoulders she wrapped it about the stranger, and before he could say a word she was gone.

In a short time strong men came and lifted the traveler and bore him gently into their village. If they were disappointed, they did not show it. They carried him to the priest, who knew how to deal with such injuries. When the priest saw the traveler he looked at him pityingly. He cut the tough fiber of the traveler's boot and bathed the injured foot in water and bound it with soothing herbs.

"I feel I hinder you," protested the traveler. "The child told me you are expecting an important guest."

"It must have been a joke of the plainsmen," answered the priest sadly. "But the villagers are prepared for a guest and will be ready to welcome you." Then he called to the men who had brought the traveler in from the forest, "Tell your neighbors that we have a guest who needs our love."

"Father," said one of the men in a low tone, "the gifts were prepared with love, and should be given. The Great One is not coming, 'tis clear. Can we not, then, give them to this traveler with the love that is in our hearts?"

"Tell the others, my son, what you would do," answered the priest with a happy light shining in his tired old eyes. "If they agree, then light the candles on the altar, and ring the bell. For One greater than all has said that this which we would do, we shall be doing unto Him. Tonight we can turn our thoughts to the Prince of Light."

The traveler lay back on the couch and closed his eyes. There was a smile on his face, but he did not speak. There was a moment of quiet, the throng before the priest's house began to shout their welcome. The church bell rang its happy welcome through the dusk and the people turned to the church with their gifts. Not even the priest saw the torn cloak of the stranger drop back, nor the chain of gold that he wore beneath.

A youth came limping into the village. His clothes were torn, and his hands were cut and bleeding. On his temple was a great bruise. He carried over his shoulder a great wedge of gray granite.

"Costah! My brother!" cried Marja, and flew to him.

"I climbed the pinnacle, little sister." Costah was breathing heavily. "Twice I fell from a crag. Often I was cut by the rough granite. The pinnacle is not smooth after all."

"But you brought the gold, Costah. The prince did not come, but there was another who needed help sorely. We are going to bless him with our love and our gifts. Bring your gift into the church brother. Hurry!"

But Costah shook his head. "It is not worthy little sister. There was no gold. The pinnacle was only granite shining in the sun. This rock is worthless. I have only the love in my heart to give." He dropped the granite at the side of the road as he spoke.

After the music and the prayers were over, quietly the people went outside. Through the open door the altar lights made a bright path for them. Suddenly the door of the priest's home opened, and the traveler came limping out. Gone was the tattered cloak. He stood before them, clad as one of themselves, save that on his breast shone a great seal. It was the seal of the king of the land and it shone in the light that streamed across his path and theirs.

"My people," said the prince, "your welcome has gladdened my heart, the more because you gave it to me, all unknown. I shall treasure your gifts and the love that you gave with them. But I have had given to me today two other gifts that you have not seen." He took from his girdle a faded, ragged little shawl that every villager there recognized.

"Marja's shawl!" they cried.

"She wrapped it around me when she ran to bring help," said the prince. "Nothing before has ever kept me so warm." He smiled into Marja's startled eyes as he spoke."

"The other gift lies there in the road at your feet. I sat by the window, Costah, my friend, and I heard all you said to your sister. I, too, have heard the legend of the plains, but I did not know there was one man in the whole world who would have faced death to bring to me the pinnacle's gold." He looked at the block of granite where it lay, and the people looked with him. As the light streamed through the open door and fell upon it, the gray block was once again tipped with gold and lay beautiful and solid in the dust of the roadway.

"This is the happiest day of my life," the visitor continued. "I want to take some of its happiness away with me, and leave some of it with you forever. This little shawl and the other gifts we will carry down the mountain when I go, but I have for you a gift also, and I will give it to you with love in my heart. It is the gift of a new church, for this little one is falling into decay. Into its altar I want you to place one of these most precious of all my gifts—Costah's granite stone from the mountain's pinnacle. Build it in and keep it to remind you of the love and service you will offer always to God and to your fellows."

"It shall be done," shouted the people. "Costah's stone shall stand among us as long as its granite endures."

And, so the story goes, there stands to this day in an almost forgotten mountain village a simple church built of the mountain rocks. In the altar close to the foot stands Costah's stone, polished and beautiful. When the sun pours through the window upon it, the surface gleams like gold, and the people smile and remember.

ELIZABETH WHITEHOUSE

Christmas

Heap on more wood!—the wind is chill;
But let it whistle as it will,
We'll keep our Christmas merry still.
Each age has deem'd the new-born year
The fittest time for festal cheer.

.　.　.　.　.　.　.　.　.

And well our Christian sires of old
Loved when the year its course had roll'd,
And brought blithe Christmas back again,
With all its hospitable train.
Domestic and religious rite
Gave honor to the holy night;
On Christmas Eve the bells were rung;
On Christmas Eve the mass was sung;

. . . .

The damsel donn'd her kirtle sheen;
The hall was dress'd with holly green;
Forth to the wood did merry-men go,
To gather in the mistletoe.

Then open'd wide the Baron's hall
To vassal, tenant, serf, and all;
Power laid his rod of rule aside,
And Ceremony doff'd his pride.

. . . .

All hail'd with uncontroll'd delight,
And general voice, the happy night,
That to the cottage, as the crown,
Brought tidings of salvation down.

SIR WALTER SCOTT

At the Castle Gate

IT WAS SUMMERTIME in the North Country, a perfect day in June. Down by the brook, children waded and gathered cowslips. Then they walked along the banks of the singing stream and collected armsful of tall bulrushes. These they hoped to sell at the castle for a few pennies to take home to their parents. Late in the afternoon they carried the rushes through the sunny meadow, stopping every so often while the littlest ones picked buttercups and daisies for their mothers.

First though, the children had to pass within the shadow of the great, gray castle that towered grimly over the plain. The two biggest, bravest boys tapped cautiously at a small gate in the rear wall and offered all the rushes for sale. The keeper of the gate bargained harshly, then flung out some small coins in payment.

Quickly, the children ran to the little huts where they lived. Not one child dared raise his eyes to see if the young earl, Sir Launfal, sat at his window high in the castle. Not one child would have dared go to the main gate. No wandering minstrel dared ask shelter in the castle for the night or offered to bring his merry songs into the castle hall. Never was a poor traveler welcomed within and sheltered and fed. Never were the castle gates opened except to lords and ladies of high degree.

On this golden June afternoon the young knight Sir Launfal did indeed sit at a window of the castle. But he did not even see the children as they went toward their poor homes. Neither did he notice a weary wayfarer struggling along the lonely road beyond the castle. Sir Launfal was lost in a daydream, one that had filled his thoughts for years. Some day he would set forth in quest of the Holy Grail, the sacred cup for which many another knight had searched. Like them, he felt that by devoting his life to this quest, he would be doing great service to the Lord Jesus.

So intent was the young knight on his plans that he did not see a beggar driven from the castle gate. He gave not a thought to a poor family with small children chased from the gate to find whatever shelter they could in the woods for the night.

Instead, Launfal made a sudden resolve. He leaped up and called his servants. When they came running, he commanded,

> "My golden spurs now bring to me,
>   And bring to me my richest mail,
>   For tomorrow I go over land and sea
>   In search of the Holy Grail."

He ordered them to spread rushes on the floor for him to sleep that night, and said, "I will not sleep on my soft bed. Perchance, tonight there may come to me some dream to guide me on my Holy Quest."

After he lay down upon the rushes, slowly his eyes grew dim and he fell into a deep sleep. As he slept a vision came to him that stirred his soul!

He dreamed it was morning and he was awakened by the lilting songs of little birds who sang as if it were the best day of summer in all the year. Quickly he made ready to start on his marvelous quest in the service of Christ.

Dressed in his coat of gilded mail, he mounted his fleet horse. Soon the drawbridge dropped with a surly clang and Sir Launfal's charger sprang through the dark archway. Young and strong, in shining armor, the proud knight flashed through the castle gateway. It was morning on hill and stream and tree, and morning in his heart.

At the castle gate he heard a moan. A leper crouched there, begging with outstretched hand. A loathing came over Sir Launfal. The flesh beneath his armor began to crawl, for this man so foul and bent rasped against the young knight's nature, and caused a blot on the summer morning. Launfal scornfully tossed the leper a piece of gold.

The leper did not raise the gold from the dusty ground, but spoke to the knight. "Better to me the poor man's crust, better the blessing of the poor. He who gives only from a sense of duty gives only worthless gold. But he who shares with kindness, even a slender gift, gives so much that the hand cannot hold it; and it cheers the heart and soul of another who was starving in darkness before."

Spurning the beggar and his words, Sir Launfal spurred his horse forward on the great search. Launfal sought the Grail in tree-shaded villages. He toiled up mountainsides, stones rolling perilously beneath the horse's hooves. He followed wild and desolate paths. Year after year after year, he traveled by land and sea, searching, searching, searching. He made his way through crowded cities searching, growing old and poor as he searched. His horse grew old and died.

Launfal was all alone. Yet, the lonely, aging man would not give up his quest. He walked the rough roads with weary, aching feet. His shining armor long since had rusted and fallen apart. On and on he went, a stranger in strange lands, suffering, searching to serve the Lord.

At last the aged knight was too feeble to go on. Sorrowfully Sir Launfal turned painfully back toward his home. Mile after endless mile, he plodded his toilsome way until, one snowy Christmastime, he drew near his castle. Through the bitter cold and snow he struggled on in the gathering darkness, longing to be within the great hall and warm himself by the Yule log and eat of the Christmas feast.

Down swept the chill wind from the mountain peak and whirled

snow on the wanderer's cheek. It carried a shiver everywhere. The brook near the castle lay frozen, glistening beneath the white stars' frosty gleams. The aged Sir Launfal pushed his way through the bulrushes that were studded with sparkling icicles.

When he came near the castle gate a merry Christmas carol floated from the hall as the door opened for a moment. He caught a glimpse of the great hall. Every rafter was entwined with ivy and holly. Through the deep gulf of the chimney, a flaming Yule log sent sparks upward like startled golden deer racing away. The hall rang with song and laughter as many guests feasted merrily. They were strangers to Sir Launfal, and as the door closed before his eyes he realized that another was now master of the castle.

Trembling with weariness, cold, and hunger, Sir Launfal tried to find shelter in the portico from the sharp wind, but the gate-keeper shouted, "Begone, old beggar!" Driven away into the bitter night, the aged man sank down outside the gateway. He could go no farther. Little did he regret that another heir had taken over his earldom; but he sorrowed that he had not found the Grail.

All night long, the ruddy glow of the Christmas lights in the hall shone through the window slits of the old castle; and ever and again came the sound of music from within. But the wind outside was bitter and sharp. It rattled the bare boughs of the trees and wailed around Sir Launfal's head, seeming to cry, "Shelterless, shelterless, shelterless."

When morning dawned at last, the sun was pale and cold. A single crow on a bleak treetop looked down at the homeless old man and cawed harshly. Sir Launfal was cold and hungry. He did not know where to go. He tried to turn his thoughts from his plight. So, drawing his threadbare cloak about him, he sought shelter from the cold and snow by remembering journeys of long ago.

From his reverie, Sir Launfal was suddenly aroused. A quavering voice cried, "For the sweet sake of Christ, I beg an alms." He beheld again the gruesome leper, horrible to look upon. This time, however, the knight did not spurn the beggar nor shrink away. Instead, his heart welled with sympathy.

Going to the leper, he spoke with true kindness. "I behold in thee an image of Christ. Thou, also, hast suffered the world's buffets and scorns, and been wounded as was he. Behold, through him, I give to thee!"

> Then the soul of the leper stood up in his eyes
> And looked at Sir Launfal, and straightway he
> Remembered in what a haughtier guise
> He had flung an alms to leprosie,
> When he girt his young life up in gilded mail
> And set forth in search of the Holy Grail.

Sad at heart, Launfal took his single crust of bread and gave the beggar half. He carried his wooden bowl to the little stream and broke the ice and brought back water for the leper to drink.

As Sir Launfal mused with downcast eyes, a light shone out. The leper no longer crouched at his side, but stood before him, shining and tall and fair and straight. And his voice that was softer than silence said.

> "Lo, it is I, be not afraid!
> In many climes, without avail,
> Thou hast spent thy life for the Holy Grail;
> Behold, it is here—this cup which thou
> Didst fill at the streamlet for me but now.

The Holy Supper is kept, indeed,
In whatso we share with another's need;
Not what we give, but what we share,
For the gift without the giver is bare;
Who gives himself with his alms feeds three,
Himself, his hungering neighbor, and me."

Then it was that the young Sir Launfal awoke from his deep sleep on his bed of rushes. Truly, a marvelous vision had come to him during the night. He sprang up and ran to tell his servants, crying, "The Grail is found here in my castle! Hang up my armor. Let it stay idle. Open wide the castle gate to everyone. Welcome the sick and the poor and the stranger."

The news spread swift on the warm June breeze; and ere that day was over the children brought to the castle hall gifts of blossoming clover and other fragrant flowers from the fields. And a ministrel wandered in with his lute and filled the hall with song.

The castle gate stands open now, and the wanderer is welcome to the hall. No longer do the tall turrets scowl, but when the first poor outcast went in at the door it seemed that the sunlit warmth of summer entered, too, and lingers there the whole year. And each poor man in the North Country shares in the earldom as much as does Sir Launfal.

JAMES RUSSELL LOWELL *(Retold)*

Hospitality
A Remembrance for Christmas

I saw a stranger yestre'en;
I put food in the eating place,
Drink in the drinking place,
Music in the listening place;
And in the sacred name of the Triune,
   He blessed myself and my house,
   My cattle and my dear ones.

And the lark said in her song,
   Often, often, often,
Goes the Christ in the stranger's guise;
   Often, often, often,
Goes the Christ in the stranger's guise.

Celtic Rune

Nanka and Marianka Make the Big Christmas Bread

MAMINKA had to go away to the city to have the good fat Bohemian doctor wrap up her hand. Aunt Pantsy was coming to stay for a while. But right now there was nobody to make Old Grampa's big Christmas bread. Maminka usually made it for him every day, because he liked it.

"Nanka!" said Marianka all of a sudden. "We must make Old Grampa's big Christmas bread!"

"Yi!" said Nanka, reaching for Maminka's red-checked apron. Then she tied her own little apron round herself. And, right away, they got out some flour and some sugar and some raisins and some nuts and some butter and two little brown eggs, to make some dough in the big yellow mixing bowl.

When the dough was made, they turned it out on the kitchen table to knead it. They kneaded it and kneaded it. And after they had kneaded it, they rolled it into some long ropes which Marianka twisted into braids—just the way Maminka always did. The braids she laid one on top of the other. Nanka patted them down, all over.

Then, both together, they put the bread into the oven, lit the stove, and closed the door.

"I hope it is going to be beautiful!" said Marianka.

"You big bread!" shouted Nanka, skipping back and forth in front of the stove. "Be beautiful!"

After a long time Marianka opened the oven door.

"Mm, Mari-an-ka!" said Nanka, looking in at the big Christmas bread.

"Mm, Nan-ka!" said Marianka.

It *was* beautiful! And shiny! And done! Very carefully, with three dish towels apiece, to keep from burning their fingers, Nanka and Marianka lifted it out of the oven and onto the kitchen table.

Marianka got down the powdered sugar and made a white snowstorm over the top of the big shiny bread. And when it was cool enough, she whispered, "Na! Let's take it to Old Grampa, wherever he is!"

Old Grampa happened to be just outside the kitchen door on the back doorsteps. But he was surprised just the same.

When Nanka came out carrying the big Christmas bread, followed by Marianka clapping her hands and singing a little Christmas song, Old Grampa could hardly believe his eyes. First he winked and then he blinked and then he said something in Bohemian.

"What does he say?" asked Nanka.

"He says he's afraid it's a dream," Marianka explained.

"Don't be afraid, Old Grampa!" said Nanka, "It's no dream!"

So Old Grampa took out his sharp knife, to find out if it tasted as good as it looked. He could hardly wait! He put his sharp knife to the bread's crust. He pushed down. He pushed again. He pressed hard. Then he grunted.

"Oof!" grunted Old Grampa. And the powdered sugar flew up like snow in the wind. Yes, it certainly was a beautiful bread! But Old Grampa's sharp knife would not cut it.

Marianka brought out all the knives that were in the kitchen. Old Grampa tried one after the other. But *no* knife would cut it! Nanka and Marianka sat down—plunk!—on each side of Old Grampa.

"You big bread!" said Nanka.

"Hard as a brick!" sighed Marianka.

After a while Old Grampa took his big red handkerchief out from his pocket. He wiped Nanka's nose and Marianka's nose. Then he put his arms round them both and told them something in Bohemian.

"What's he say?" asked Nanka, sniffling.

"He says he knows what!" explained Marianka, sniffling too. "He's going to tie a long string round it and hang it up on his wall, because it's too beautiful to eat, anyway. He's just going to keep on looking at it, forever and ever!"

"Ho-o!" giggled Nanka, quite suddenly. "Too beautiful to eat!" Marianka giggled, too.

Old Grampa wiped their noses once more. Then he put his red handkerchief back into his pocket, laid the big bread on the top step with all the knives and went shuffling away to find a string long enough to hang it by.

"Too beautiful to eat—na!—just think, Nanka!" said Marianka, taking a deep breath after Old Grampa had disappeared. Nanka took a deep breath, too.

Then they smiled at each other, as proud as proud could be!

ELIZABETH ORTON JONES

O the Morn

Sweet the song, the happy happy song,
   Precented at His birth,
And caught up by the heav'nly throng,
   "Good-will, and Peace on Earth!"

So, my boys, my bonny, bonny boys,
   To Bethlem off be we
But, pray you, shun whate'er annoys
   The Babe on Mary's knee.

An Early Carol

Tree of Birds

They must have suddenly remembered,
in that blizzard-blown December,
when food was scarce and singing hard,
the mountain-ash in our silver yard.

That Day-before-Christmas afternoon
when the snowstorm stopped and dusk came soon,
they flew into our snowy tree
with wild and happy minstrelsy.

Each Chickadee, black-capped and merry,
feasted on cool and scarlet berries,
and till the early stars grew strong
gave us a Christmas tree of song!

FRANCES FROST

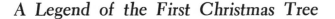

A Legend of the First Christmas Tree

THE GREAT LONELINESS of the forest pressed in around a small silent band of men huddled close to a flickering fire. The night wind sighed through the trees, and one man sighed with it. Others glanced quickly about, fearful that wild tribesmen might be lurking behind the trees ready to spring upon the travelers. For, in those deep forests of Germany in the eighth century, there still lived dangerous pagan tribes who were hostile to strangers, and who made living sacrifices.

Boniface, the leader of the serious-faced men by the fire, spoke comfortingly, "Good Christian brothers, take heart. It is true that these woods are frightening to us who grew up in comfortable homes on the open English moors. There we could see nearby villages and church spires, and our neighbors were friendly. But, let us not forget that if Christian teachers had not come to our homeland years ago and taught our ancestors that God is the loving Father of all people we, also, might still be wild pagans."

He poked up the fire, and its light glowed on his strong, young face and bright, kindly eyes. The men in the circle leaned forward, watching him with new hope and courage. They had pledged themselves to bring the teachings of Jesus to the wild Saxon tribes who roamed these forests; and, with Boniface for their leader, they would be loyal and brave.

They had been traveling many days through strange land watching for a hunter who was being sent from a tiny village where there was a monastery. The Christian brothers who had come there to teach a few years before had arranged to send this hunter as a guide for Boniface and his men. But the hunter had not come, and some felt lost as they settled down to sleep.

During the night came a sound that roused them. "Boniface!" the call was far off, but clear. The men called back—relieved that their guide had finally come. Before long they could make out a shadowy figure coming toward them through the trees. The man called, "God"s blessings to you, good brothers," and they went forward to meet him. Across his shoulder was slung a large bow, and from the belt of his hunting shirt hung a quiver full of long arrows. But the travelers were not afraid for he was welcoming them.

As he reached the firelight he said, "You do not know how wonderful it is for us and our children and all the children of the future that you have come to our land to teach the ways of Jesus!"

They sat by the fire talking until dawn. He told them that before Christian missionaries had come to his people, his family lived as part of a pagan tribe. "We were afraid of evil spirits in the trees and in the mist, in the rivers and drinking pools. We offered human sacrifices so these spirits wouldn't harm us."

He lowered his voice talking almost to himself, but they leaned forward and heard every word. "My father was a headman in our tribe. His grandson (my only boy) was marked to be slain as a sacrifice at the Wotan Oak of Geisner when the tribes gathered there in December. But God was good to us. He sent us teachers who brought us light and hope instead of dark fear."

In the days that followed, Boniface and his men followed their guide among the thousands of trees that shut out daylight. Night after night, weary and often hungry, they wrapped themselves in

their cloaks and lay down to sleep, in danger of attack by wild animals or wild tribesmen. Often, before they slept they talked about the terrible Wotan oak. It was far, far beyond. But some December Boniface planned to reach it when the tribes gathered. That would be an awful time, they all knew.

However, before that time came, there was much work to be done. They must visit monasteries and schools that already had been established, and help wherever they could.

At last, late one afternoon they came upon a clearing in the forest and beheld before them a wooden chapel with several small houses clustered nearby. At sight of their guide, a blond-haired girl of about eight called "Father!" She grasped the hand of a little one close by and they came running to greet their father. The hunter hugged his children. Then he introduced them proudly to Boniface and the other men.

Soon, from all the houses people came out to welcome them. A frail, elderly man in the plain robe of a Christian monk hurried from the chapel, exclaiming, "God be praised! You have reached here at last. We need you in this vast forest land."

That night the tired travelers found shelter, warmth, food, and friendliness in various homes in this little Christian village in the forest. Boniface was lodged in the hut of the hunter who had guided them. Each evening after supper he and the family talked and worked together—whittling arrows, mending fish nets, even pounding grain.

He looked at the oldest son, whose strong hands were mending a fish net by the firelight. Such fine youths as this were slain yearly at the Wotan Oak! Boniface asked, "Why do tribesmen believe the god of light and fire from the sun lives in the Wotan Oak during dark December days?"

The hunter explained. "Perhaps because dried oak sticks, when rubbed together, make a spark and kindle fire faster than wood of other trees. The people are afraid this god of light and fire will not send back the sunshine unless they give him a very special sacrifice."

The little girl, who had been resting on a blanket, sat up straight, saying, "But we love December. It is the happiest time of the year —the Christ Child's birthday time. When you were a boy, did you have a Christmas feast as we do, and sing and light your house, and welcome strangers?"

"We did, indeed," Boniface told her. "We loved Christmastime. We children gathered holly and evergreen branches and decorated our homes. One Christmas some traveling Christian brothers came to my father's home. They helped us decorate the great hall with fragrant Christmas greens; and that evening by the fireside one played a lute and we all sang Christmas songs. Later they told us that we should be thankful that we celebrated Jesus' birthday in December instead of holding ceremonies like those at the Wotan Oak."

Boniface looked around at this family whom he had come to love. Then he said to the little girl, "Even though I was a boy then not many years older than you, I made up my mind I would do everything I could to help people in the forest tribes enjoy Christmas and all that it means to the world."

The hunter cried, "First the terrible power of the Thunder Oak, the Wotan Oak, must be broken. It must be destroyed before the people's eyes so that they can see that no dreadful god lives in it."

"Some day, I shall cut down that oak, and free the people of its spell," Boniface vowed.

Several years passed before Boniface could make the perilous journey to the Oak tree. During those years he was called twice to Rome, and was made Bishop of Germany. This was a great responsibility, for he had to work even harder building more new churches and monasteries and training teachers and workers.

Then, one December, Boniface learned that an unusually large number of tribesmen were to go to the Wotan Oak, and several of the finest youths were to be killed. So Boniface and three monks went to the village of their friend, the hunter-guide, and asked the location of the oak tree.

"We go to stop the sacrifice," declared Boniface to the hunter and his family.

For a moment the room was hushed. Then the hunter stood up brave and tall. "I will guide you. The pagan high priest has called the tribes to meet at the Oak five nights from now. We must start in the morning. There is no time to waste if we would reach the Wotan Oak in time to save the lives of the boys, and show the people the tree is powerless."

The older son came and stood by his father. "I shall go and help, too. I want those girls and boys to be able to grow up as I did, and not fear the evil spirits in the mist and the darkness, in rivers and in trees."

The mother came and put her hand on her son's shoulder. She was pale and frightened as she looked from her good husband to her good son, yet she spoke bravely. "You may all be killed on this dangerous mission. Yet, we will trust God to be with you."

Next morning before dawn the men set out on their journey. Icy wind bit their faces as they plunged into the dark, lonely forest. Mysterious mists rose like eerie spirits. The boy whispered, "Some people think those mists are ghosts of fierce warriors slain in battle, riding to the home of the gods."

Boniface replied, "We must try to help them understand that God is not a God of fighting and bloodshed, but a loving Father who wants to protect his children."

On and on they went until they came to a foaming torrent, cascading down a hillside—too wide to leap, too swift to wade. With ringing strokes of his axe the hunter felled a tree, and with it the men bridged the roaring stream. Onward they struggled, brushing past countless small fir trees, snow-tipped.

Then at last they reached a clearing where several houses stood. The men hoped to rest and get warm, but the village was deserted, and last night's snowfall had covered all footprints.

The hunter said, "The pagan high priest lives here. He has already led his people toward the Oak. We must hurry!"

They struggled on through the darkness as long as they could, then slept exhausted in a thicket of small evergreen trees. The evergreens reminded Boniface of trees that he and his friends took indoors at Christmastime when they were boys in England. He lay awake, very cold, remembering his home and the warm, cheerful hall, where fragrant Christmas greens gleamed in the firelight. But he told himself that he had chosen to leave his home and all its Christmas joys, in the hope of bringing the true joy and light of Christmas to the Saxon tribes.

Day after day they pushed on through the forest, straining for speed so as not to be too late. Once in a while, footprints in the snow led from side paths into the path they now followed. On the fifth afternoon the snowy path ahead widened and showed the marks of many feet. As they pushed forward, the hunter whispered, "We draw near the Thunder Oak. The sacrifice will be made at nightfall!"

Two of their small group stood still, pale with fear. Boniface's heart was pounding as he prayed aloud, "Heavenly Father, give us courage!" Together the band moved ahead swiftly, fighting their fears as they drew near to the Oak.

Darkness fell fast. Ahead they glimpsed the flicker of a fire surrounded by dark silent figures. Boniface heard a sob. Near him a woman wept, half hidden by a fir tree. At sight of them she fled.

"Quick Boniface," gasped the hunter, "The pagan priest's knife is raised."

Boniface called out in a loud voice, "Fear not; for behold, I bring you good tidings of great joy, which shall be to all people." He walked swiftly into the circle of light and stood beside a tall blonde youth who was bound with ropes.

Amazed by the sudden appearance of Boniface and by his courage, everyone stood still. Then he talked with the people and priest as a friend would, who had brought them good news. While he talked, he cut the cords that bound the young man. No one stopped him. When Boniface boldly advanced to the Thunder Oak, they shrank back.

He swung his axe and shouted, "This tree has no power over you. All power rests in God, the father of us all."

He cut the trunk a resounding blow. Some people screamed and hid their eyes. Some started to run in terror. But no dreadful spirit appeared. Then they watched, fascinated, and slowly moved away from the tree so it would not hit them when it fell. Some were beginning to lose fear. What he had told them made them hopeful; and he was very brave. As the axe chopped deeper into the Thunder Oak, the sound rang through the forest.

At last the mighty tree crashed to the ground. Almost at once a beautiful song sounded in the winter night. Boniface's companions were singing, "Glory to God in the highest; and on earth peace, good will toward men."

Some persons lifted their children to their shoulders so they could hear the music better and see the singers. They watched while Boniface walked toward a perfect little fir tree growing near where the Oak had fallen.

He touched it, saying, "See how this little evergreen points to the sky. Call it the tree of the Christ Child. Take it into your homes. Do not celebrate God's power in the forest with wicked rites; but celebrate his power in the sacredness of your homes with laughter and love, with peace and good will."

He smiled at a wide-eyed little child, and told them all, "The time is coming when in each home in the north, on the birthday of Christ the whole family will gather around the fir tree to commemorate the day and to glorify God."

Once more his companions sang, "Glory to God in the highest, and on earth peace, good will toward men." Slowly, gently, Boniface led some of the people to join in the singing.

Boniface stayed among the various tribes for some time and taught them. Stories about Jesus spread throughout the land; and before many years more and more people celebrated his birthday joyfully, decorating their homes, singing beautiful songs, giving gifts, and sharing the Christmas feast with the poor and with strangers.

From Germany the happy custom of decorating evergreen trees for Jesus' birthday has entered many homes around the world. Instead of fearing December darkness, people now look through its mysterious beauty toward the stars, remembering the star that led wise men toward the Light of the World. And often on their Christmas trees they place a lighted star for the Christ Child.

MILDRED C. LUCKHARDT

Voices in the Mist

The time draws near the birth of Christ:
  The moon is hid, the night is still;
  The Christmas bells from hill to hill
Answer each other in the mist.

Four voices of four hamlets round,
  From far and near, on mead and moor,
  Swell out and fail, as if a door
Were shut between me and the sound;

Each voice four changes on the wind,
  That now dilate, and now decrease,
  Peace and good will, good will and peace,
Peace and good will, to all mankind.

ALFRED, LORD TENNYSON

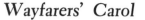

Wayfarers' Carol

Snow is falling o'er the hills:
Those who tarry, if God wills,
   Home may win.
Wanderers abroad, and lost,
Footsore, and mayhap storm-tossed,
   Far from kin—
   Look up, pray!
On Christmas Eve, of old they say,
Cometh help to light the way!

Every twisting thorny tree
Within is lit so fierily;
   Shadowless,
And sheltering from all that's wild
His candle, comes a little child.
   Loveliness
   Beyond compare
Dwells about Him; and most dear
The yellow light that He doth bear.

Straightly to His feet hangs down
His shining crocus-coloured gown;

120

Round His head
A circle of immortal light
Whirls with swiftness infinite;
    At His tread
    Blossoms spring;
Wandering brothers, let us sing
To this Youngling's journeying:
    Gloria, Gloria
    In excelsis Deo!

J. MACLEOD

For Christmas

Now not a window small or big
But wears a wreath of holly sprig;
Nor any shop too poor to show
Its spray of pine or mistletoe.
Now city airs are spicy-sweet
With Christmas trees along each street,
Green spruce and fir whose boughs will hold
Their tinsel balls and fruits of gold.
Now postman pass in threes and fours
Like bent, blue-coated Santa Claus.
Now people hurry to and fro
With little girls and boys in tow,
And not a child but keeps some trace
Of Christmas secrets in his face.

RACHEL FIELD

Angels from Oberammergau

A CLEAR STARLIT SKY stretched over the snowy streets of Boston, as Maria and Karl crunched through the snow with their father on the Christmas Eve walk they took every year. All the way along they had stopped to look in windows at Christmas trees and at creches. They stood long, admiring one creche, with figures much like those in theirs at home.

"Probably from Oberammergau," murmured Maria, standing on tiptoe to see. Karl nodded. Their grandfather had carved many such beautiful little figures while their father was a little boy in the lovely village of Oberammergau far across the sea. Sometimes, especially at Christmas when they were fixing their creche, they felt that their parents were a bit homesick for the childhood home.

This Christmas Eve, as they walked along Charles Street where the shops were, Maria and Karl kept hoping to find some special gift for their father. But the wind was blowing cold, and they saw no such gift for him.

By the time they reached Miss Abbott's gift shop where they were to buy paper and ribbon they were glad to go inside and get warm. While they selected what Mother wanted, Father went to the back of the shop to look around. They found him there, holding in his hand a small angel carved out of light honey-colored wood. He was gazing intently at the angel. They moved closer to see.

With its head thrown back and its right hand on its hip, the angel was blowing a tiny delicate horn. From its shoulders came two jaunty little wings and its hair was tightly curled, amazingly real looking. The angel was not more than four inches high, most exquisitely carved, full of life and grace and motion.

Maria cried, "Father, how lovely! Where did it come from?"

They knew before he answered, "Oberammergau. There is a whole orchestra of angels. One plays the flute, another a violin, another a drum and cymbals, another holds a roll of music and is singing, another has a tiny baton, and so on."

"Oh," exclaimed Miss Abbott, "you know them all. I had them, but sold them fast. I liked this one best. I can't think how it ever was left."

"We ought to buy it for our creche," declared Maria.

Father turned it slowly with expert fingers, and shook his head. "I am sure it is too expensive for us. Such works of art are made by carvers who have had years of training and experience. I am glad there are people who can afford to buy them, but families like ours have to be content with admiring them."

Miss Abbot understood. However, she said, "Mr. Bayer it is so late now, if you want it you may have it for five dollars. It was six and a half."

She walked away to give him time to think, and he stood still, holding the angel and looking away into space. "He's thinking about Oberammergau and the happy days he spent as a boy learning from his father how to carve," thought Maria. "He remembers skiing home from school down the snowy road and watching the lights of the houses, glowing yellow and warm through the dusk, and music floating out when doors were opened, as he has often told us."

Karl was thinking, "Father is a good American, but there is

always a homesick place inside him."

Suddenly a little smile broke over Father's face. Both children expected him to say to Miss Abbott, "I'll take the angel." Instead they were very disappointed when he put it back on the self and turned away.

When Maria asked, "Aren't you going to take it for our creche?" Father shook his head and said the angel would blow its horn just as loudly and sweetly in an American creche as in one made in Oberammergau as theirs was.

"Come, your mother will be wondering where we are," he added. He thanked Miss Abbott and wished her a merry Christmas and led the way home. They were all very quiet as they walked together through the snow. At just about the same time Maria and Karl had just about the same idea. They hurried along, eager to tell it to each other when Father was not around.

In the coat closet, while hanging up their coats, they were able to whisper it. Then they rushed downstairs to tell Mother.

"There's a carved angel from Oberammergau in Miss Abbott's shop, and Father likes it very much, and could we take the money out of our banks and get it for him?" Maria said it all in one breath and then had to stop for air.

So Karl explained. "It cost five dollars, and could we run and buy it before the shop closes? He really likes it Mother, and you know how he's always trying to do things for us that we like."

Mother clapped her hands. "Why don't we all three take money from our banks to by the angel for Father?"

They were delighted. Maria said, "We'll run down for it now. Mother, you try to think of some way in which you can put it at the creche after Father goes to bed. We want him to see it there when you open the door in the morning."

They quickly planned how to get back to the shop without Father's suspecting. So Mother called loudly, "Oh, I forgot cherries for the pudding. Maria and Karl, please run and get some."

They scampered upstairs for their coats, got their money and were off before Father noticed. The clock in the hall said quarter of six, so they ran all the way through the biting cold to Miss Abbott's shop. What if she closed it before they arrived?

Panting, they reached it at last and ran in. Before they could tell her what they wanted, she came to meet them carrying a small box, gaily wrapped. "Here is the angel with the horn," she said smiling. "I knew you would be back for it after you saw your father standing there holding it.

The children could hardly wait for tomorrow morning when Father would first see this new figure in the creche.

When they went to bed that night they were still thinking about how surprised Father would be.

Maria did not know how long she had slept when a sound from the basement kitchen two floors below awakened her. Somebody was yodeling. Then she heard her mother laughing and saying, "Ssh!"

Putting on her bathrobe and slippers, Maria went softly downstairs. Yodeling and singing started again, this time softly, and with it came the sound of dancing feet. She peered over the stair rail. There in the kitchen were her mother and father singing and dancing and laughing, and trying not to make much noise. Mother wore her bright green dirndl skirt and white blouse with short puffed sleeves that she had brought from Oberammergau. Father wore his leather trousers and embroidered suspenders. They were doing one of the old dances.

Suddenly Mother stopped, saying, "It's past three o'clock. We must get some sleep."

Maria scooted quietly back to bed before they saw her. She kept wondering, if it was so late, how Mother would get the angel into the creche without Father's seeing it first.

Next morning before daylight their little brother Toni awoke them all, singing "Away in a Manger." Everyone sprang out of bed and hurried down to eat breakfast quickly. Maria and Karl wondered if Mother was able to place the angel without Father seeing it.

At last, Mother went upstairs to the living room to light the tree. Then when they heard her singing "O Tannenbaum," they joined in, and climbed the stairs. Mother was waiting for them at the door of the living room. Father opened it and they all surged through.

Somehow, they all looked first toward the creche and then stopped short. There was not one angel, but TWO angels carved out of pale, honey-colored wood. One was the angel blowing the horn, and on the opposite side was an angel exactly the same size and color, playing an accordion. Her body seemed to sway and bend with the music, and she looked intent on drawing from the accordion lilting music as an offering to the Christ Child. Amazed, Karl and Maria

went and touched the angel. Karl turned it around slowly, looking at the accordion. "You made it, Father!" cried Maria.

Then Mother spoke. "I've kept secrets for the whole family all night."

Everyone started asking questions. Father wanted to know how the twins got the angel with the horn before the shop closed. Karl asked "How could you ever make the accordion angel just the right size?" Maria asked, "Mother, how did you get both angels to the creche without any of us seeing you?"

Then Mother told the whole story. "The idea for making the angel with the accordion came to your father while he held the other angel in Miss Abbott's shop. He wondered if his father might have made that angel with the horn. Then he remembered his own tools in an old chest with several small pieces of fine wood he had brought from home."

Smiling, Father explained, "I decided to try to carve an angel for the orchestra and decided that an accordion would be easier to carve than some other instrument. I thought you children never would settle down in bed before I could start to work. Then I put on my old leather trousers that I always wore in the carving shop. While I worked, your Mother dressed in her girlhood clothes and carried all the presents into the living room and arranged them under the tree."

Mother laughed. "Your father was still carving when I finished. So I made him coffee and sandwiches. He ate without stopping to think what he ate and went on working, hour after hour. I went and sat in a big chair and dozed off, dreaming of the Christmas Eve procession in Oberammergau winding through the village, with a lighted star carried in the lead. Next thing I knew your father was calling me to see the angel he had carved."

She stopped a moment while they all looked at it again. Then she said, "I thought it was the most beautiful little figure I ever had seen."

We danced for joy—our old village dances," added Father. "After that we went upstairs and placed the accordion angel in the creche. I could hardly wait until you children discovered her this morning. And now I have a wonderful surprise from you, the angel with the horn. That is a real Christmas treasure." He picked it up and looked at it as he had done in the gift shop.

"Mother," asked Karl, "how did you get it into the creche without Father's knowing?"

"I hid the angel with the horn in the cookie jar until Father started for bed. Then I quickly took it and set it in the creche."

"So now we have two new angels in our home," said Father, holding one in each hand. "As I worked on the accordion angel I thought that hidden away in the piece of wood was an angel that never saw Oberammergau, just as you children never saw that place. But the wood she is made of and the hand that carved her came from Oberammergau, so she is a special kind of angel, bringing together our old life and our new one. You were born here and belong here, but in you is something precious that you must always be proud of which your mother and I brought as a gift to America."

The twins nodded. They understood and they were very happy.

ELIZABETH DURYEA (*adapted*)

Christmas Bells

I heard the bells on Christmas Day
Their old familiar carols play,
   And wild and sweet
   The words repeat,
Of "Peace on earth, good will to men!"

And thought how, as the day had come,
The belfries of all Christendom
   Had rolled along
   The unbroken song,
Of "Peace on earth, good will to men!"

Till ringing, singing, on its way,
The world revolved from night to day,—
    A voice, a chime,
    A chant sublime,
Of "Peace on earth, good will to men!"

And in dispair I bowed my head,
There is no peace on earth I said,
    For hate is strong
    And mocks the song
Of "Peace on earth, good will to men."

Then pealed the bells more loud and deep;
    "God is not dead; nor doth he sleep!
    The wrong shall fail, the right prevail,
With peace on earth, good will to men!"

HENRY WADSWORTH LONGFELLOW

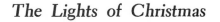

The Lights of Christmas

THERE WERE neither clocks nor calendars in the small village in India where Jaswunt lived. It did not matter much because he did not need them. The sun told him when to get up and when to go to bed. He knew it was spring when he helped Father plant the seeds and autumn when he helped harvest the grain and store it in clay jars.

And Jaswunt knew when it was Christmas! Because then he and Father made preparations together for the Great Day.

As Christmas drew near, Father would say, "It's time now for us to go to the potter's for new clay saucers for the Christmas lights." So they would go to the market ten miles away and buy silver squares for icing the Christmas cakes, colored paper for Christmas decorations, and powder to make paints for Mother's Christmas pictures.

On the day before the Great Day the minister, Padre Sahib, would come from the village beyond and meet the children under the mango tree. Father, always came, too, and listened with Jaswunt to the story of the Baby Jesus and sang with him the shepherd's song.

But this year as Christmas came closer, things were different. Very different!

Father was not at home, and seven-year-old Jaswunt was worried.

This year after grain harvest, Father had said, "I'm going to the city to find work in the mill."

When Jaswunt asked, "How can I get ready for Christmas without you?" Father had promised, "I'll be home in time. I'll bring money for the hundred Christmas lights. I'll have money for everything!"

Father had put his bundle on his back and started on the long walk to the market town where he took the train to the distant city.

Now Christmas would soon be here. Jaswunt knew it was time to get ready for it, but Mother said, "We must wait for Father. What can we do when we have no money?"

One morning Jaswunt told his mother, "Ram Singh says his uncle is going to market to sell his new cart wheels. Please let me ride with him."

Mother consented. "If you are careful, you may go."

Before they left, Jaswunt helped to lift the new wheels into the cart. After the oxen were hitched into place, he and Ram Singh's uncle climbed up for their long ride.

At the market Jaswunt helped to unload the wheels and to set them around the stall for buyers to examine. Afterward he wandered from one booth to another. In one he spied the squares of silver and the colored paper and powder for paints.

"If only Father were here, we could buy them now," he thought. In his own pocket was not one anna—only the roasted lentils Mother had put there for his lunch. How could he ever make ready for Christmas all by himself?

Jaswunt found a shady place and ate his lunch. Soon he saw Ram Singh's uncle on the cart. It must be time to start home!

Jaswunt hopped onto the cart. Ram Singh's uncle seemed in no hurry, but said, "Hold out your hands." Into Jaswunt's open palms he dropped some coins. "I sold my wheels and made a fair profit. These are for you. You earned them helping me."

Jaswunt looked at the coins a moment and his fingers closed quickly over them.

"Oh, thank you!" he cried, and in a flash he was on his way to the booth where he had seen the colored powder. He handed the coins to the man there. "Please give me as many colors as these will buy. Now my mother can paint the pictures for the Great Day!"

At home, Jaswunt handed the package to Mother. "We do not need to wait for Father. I can plan for Christmas."

That evening a knock came at the gate. Jaswunt rushed to answer it. Perhaps it was Father. But no! Father would walk right in!

Outside stood the son of the village headman. He had a letter for Mother. "The mail carrier came through the village about a week ago and left this for you, but my father has been too busy to send it until now."

Mother told Jaswunt, "Tomorrow you will take the letter to Padre Sahib. He will read it and tell us what Father says."

It was early when Jaswunt started across the fields to the minister's home in the village beyond.

"Your letter brings good news, "Padre Sahib said after reading it. "Your father is in good health. He will come home the day before the Great Day. He says you are to go ahead with the Christmas plans."

"How long before my father comes?" Jaswunt asked.

"The sun will set twice," Padre Sahib told him.

When Mother heard, she said, "I will begin the Christmas paintings tomorrow. At least, they will be ready."

Jaswunt begged, "Let me try to get the lights, Mother. I'll go to the potter's tomorrow."

At the potter's shop Jaswunt almost sang his words. "One hundred clay saucers for our Christmas lights! Father said one hundred."

The potter turned angrily from his wheel. "Why do you come so late? The Great Day is almost here. I have much work to do. Where is your money?"

Jaswunt explained, "When my father comes from the city for the Great Day, he will pay you."

The potter was not pleased. "Pay me now," he demanded crossly.

Jaswunt could not speak for disappointment. He turned to leave. The potter suddenly pointed to some chipped and uneven saucers. "Take those. They are of no use to me. You may have them without paying."

Jaswunt lifted the saucers carefully and carried them to his courtyard at home. He found there were fifty.

Next he went to the oil presser and asked for oil. The oil presser patted his head. "My lad, it would not be Christmas without plenty of oil for your lights. You may have some. Your father will pay. I do not worry."

He put Jaswunt's empty jar under the opening in the press and let oil drip slowly into it.

At home again Jaswunt put the oil beside the saucers. He hurried to the cotton field. The farmer told him, "Take only as much as you need. Such a small amount I gladly give you."

Jaswunt bent over the white snowballs popping from their thick brown pods and picked a little from one and from another, until he had a double handful of the fluffy fibers.

Jaswunt reached home and found Ram Singh waiting with colored paper sheets. "Your court must have waving pennants," Ram Singh said. He stayed and helped Jaswunt cut the paper into pretty shapes.

Together they pasted them to long strings and hung them across the courtyard.

Jaswunt called to Mother, "See! They're waving a welcome to Father."

Mother answered, "The paintings on the floor and walls welcome him, too."

The boys came and stood beside the white design Mother had made on the ground in front of the door. On the wall there was a star and a manger. They watched as Mother added the pictures of the Wise Men riding on their camels.

The next morning, Jeswunt put on clean white pants. Mother brought her wedding scraf from the tin box in honor of Father's return.

But still Father did not come.

In the afternoon Jaswunt went to the mango tree. He listened to the minister tell the story of the Baby Jesus, and he sang the shepherd's song.

> *In the skies on that dark night*
> *The shepherds saw the shining light*
> *And found the Babe all wrapped in white.*

Still Father did not come.

Toward evening Jaswunt went many times to look out the gate. Each time he told Mother, "Surely Father will be here to help fill the lamps."

When Father did not come, Jaswunt poured the oil into the fifty saucers, rolled the long cotton wicks for them, climbed along the roof, the gate, the courtyard wall, and set the lamps in place ready to light.

At sunset the smoke from many fires cooking the evening meal rose over the village. The lumbering buffaloes, the clumsy cows, the scuffling feet of children, the oxen's bells sounded along the narrow paths and cart tracks. Every creature moved slowly to its home for the night, but Father did not come.

Jaswunt heard the gay voices of Ram Singh and his other friends as they scrambled along the roofs of their houses and on tops of gates and walls to light their many lamps. He could wait no longer. He climbed from wall to roof and lighted his lamps, too.

Again he went to the gate. Again he looked far down the lighted path. In the distance a tall figure turned into the village from the country road. It was Father!

Jaswunt ran to meet him. "Oh, Father, I'm glad you have come!"

Father's big hand closed tightly around Jaswunt's small one, and together they walked home to Mother.

"There were no carts along the road today to give me a ride, so

I walked all the way," Father told them. "When night came, it was hard to follow the path. Suddenly through the darkness I saw the lamps. The lights of Christmas guided me home."

Father looked at all the signs of Christmas. From his bundles he took the silver squares and the money he had promised and a comb for Mother's hair and a new cap for Jaswunt.

Jaswunt smiled at Father. "You are home! Now we are ready for the Great Day!"

ELIZABETH ALLSTROM

A Little Child

A little Child,
  A shining star.
A stable rude,
  The door ajar.

Yet in that place,
  So crude, forlorn,
The Hope of all
  The world was born.

Author Unknown

Day Dawn in the Heart

'Tis not enough that Christ was born
  Beneath the star that shone,
And brings the day of love and good,
  Within a golden zone.

He must be born within the heart
  Before He finds a throne,
And brings the day of love and good,
  The reign of Christlike brotherhood.

Author Unknown

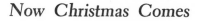

Now Christmas Comes

Now, THE DAY before Christmas, Miss Hickory felt that something of portent was in the air. Not a feeling that could be put into words, or even worked out in her mind. Nothing was changed, but the fields and the forest seemed expectant. Snow lay deep, but it was criss-crossed and mapped by the imprint of small hurrying feet, rabbits, winter birds, and deer. The laurel, whose secret hopes keep it green and fresh all winter, pushed up through the snow asking to be made into Christmas wreaths. The long green fingers of the pine tree held little snowballs, trimming itself for Christmas. Small straight hemlock and spruce trees crowded one another begging to be Christmas trees. Scarlet winter berries blended with the laurel to help in making the Christmas wreaths. And the creeping pine lay bright underneath the snow for twining into garlands.

Miss Hickory remembered last Christmas. She had lived then on the kitchen window sill of the Old Place. There, she had sniffed mince pies, turkey, and Christmas pudding, the Christmas tree in the parlor, and boiling molasses taffy. She had been given a tiny green hemlock shoot as a Christmas tree for her corncob house, and a new little gingham apron. But her life was so changed now that last Christmas was only the dimmest memory. (The family had moved from the Old Place and Crow had flown with her to this new home of hers, a snug nest in the crotch of an apple tree.) She skated and coasted about her pleasant winter world, nibbling bark and rose-hips, sticking a laurel leaf in her hat to replace the trimming Squirrel had tweaked off, and giving little thought, since she had no Old Farmer's Almanac, to the season.

That was why Miss Hickory did not believe Squirrel. He dashed up-boughs to her nest as it began to be dusk. "Full moon tonight, Miss Hickory," he announced. "Bright moonlight for Christmas Eve. You mustn't go to bed too early. Stay up for the celebration."

"What celebration?" Miss Hickory pulled her hat down tightly. Even now, after so many weeks, she did not really trust Squirrel.

"In the barn," he told her. "Something wonderful happens there every Christmas Eve at midnight. My mother took me over last Christmas to see it. Only we animals and the winged creatures see it. Large and small, wild and tame, of the earth or with God, we all go over to the barn to watch for it, and no one is afraid of those larger than himself.'"

"I have outgrown bedtime stories," Miss Hickory said crossly as she tucked her covers close about her feet. "You go, Squirrel, if you believe all this nonsense."

"The wonder on Christmas Eve is this," Squirrel continued, not noticing her remark, "In one of the barn mangers, the animal to whom it belongs finds the wonder. In the fresh grain of his manger, at midnight tonight, there will be a small hollow, although the straw and oats were freshly laid and not touched. It will be the shape of a baby's head and body. Do you know what a baby is, Miss Hickory?" he asked anxiously.

"I have seen them, but never in a barn in the dead of winter," she said sharply. "Nor have you," she snapped.

"I assure you that I saw Christmas Eve in the barn." Squirrel wrinkled his little gray forehead, sorry not to be believed.

"Just a dream that you had last night after eating too many nuts. Oh, I hear you day after day, night after night, cracking, eating." But he would not be silenced.

Then all the animals, the barn creatures and the wild creatures, see the wonder too. They crowd around the manger and—"

"Posh!" said Miss Hickory. "I have heard enough of your fancy talk. Get down-boughs, home!"

"You'll be sorry." Squirrel felt that he had been insulted. He rapped Mis Hickory's head so hard with a paw that her hat went askew. "Hardheaded!" he said as he left her.

That was coming to be a familiar description of her, Miss Hickory thought. But the fact that she had a nut for a head did make new ideas difficult for her mind to grasp. She was coming to realize that fact.

"I'll have a good night's rest and go over to the barn in the morning," she thought. "Then I can see whatever there is to see."

So on Christmas Eve Miss Hickory went to sleep early and she slept soundly until a loud sweet chiming awoke her. Like elfin bells the frosted twigs and icicles that covered her tree clashed and tinkled and rang out merry tunes. As her tree chimed, all the other trees joined in the chorus until the orchard shook and thrilled with carols. Miss Hickory sat up in bed, and the Christmas Eve moonlight on the snow was so dazzling that she rubbed her eyes, got out of bed, and went farther up-boughs to see what it was all about. As soon as she reached the top she understood that something extraordinary was taking place.

Down from the peak of Temple Mountain, into its lee and passing through the orchard in the direction of the barn, Miss Hickory saw a strange procession. Flying ahead like a courier came a crow, but not Crow whom Miss Hickory knew, for this one was white. Follow-

ing the white crow came the robins with sprays of holy in their bills and the bluebirds carrying laurel leaves. Fawn came next. Doe, his mother, was beside him. The two, Fawn and Doe, stepped lightly, and in time to the orchard chimes. They came slowly, looking neither toward the woods nor the fields, for they were not afraid.

Miss Hickory chuckled when she saw Cock-Pheasant, a brilliant painting as his beautful tail feathers trailed the snow. He joined the Christmas parade at High-Mowing, where he had called at the headquarters of the Ladies' Aid Society for Hen-Pheasants. She walked in the procession at a respectful distance behind Cock. But Miss Hickory held her breath as the peacocks came in handsome array down the mountainside, tails of jeweled color or white laces spread in great fans. Nightingales came singing; green and gold parrots flew past in pairs with palm leaves in their bills; light-footed goats with bells at their throats danced. When she saw the camels

marching, tall and majestic in silk trappings, she was frightened. But the home creatures mingled fearlessly among these others from far away. . . . The large ones in the procession stepped carefully so as not to harm the small ones. . . .

Miss Hickory felt dizzy as if she were losing her mind. When she felt warm breathing on her neck there, up-boughs, she almost fell out of the tree. But it was only Squirrel, who fairly barked in her ear:

"What did I tell you, Miss Hickory? Now will you believe me? I am off now. You had better hurry or you will be late."

"There is no need for haste." Miss Hickory did, however, scramble down-boughs. "The barn will wait for me." But Squirrel did not hear her. She was really somewhat alarmed at being alone on so splendid a night, and she almost coasted down her tree from one icy branch to another. Having reached the ground, she took her place at the end of the procession. An odd little creature with human hands, face, and a long curling tail was just ahead of her. He walked upright. Monkey turned to look at Miss Hickory, then raised one little hand toward the sky where a great blazing star in the East now outshone the moon. Then he sped on.

"All contrary to the Almanac," Miss Hickory said to herself. "No stars are bright in the full of the moon."

But she too, small and alone, trailed on in the light of the Christmas star until she reached the barn.

At once she found that she had waited too long. The barn door was opened and inside, the home animals, Cow, Twin-Heifers, Old Horse, the fowls, the sheep and lambs, crowded. Mr. T. Willard-Brown, the cat, wearing a smartly tied bow of red ribbon sat primly beside a circle of gray-gowned mice, not even sniffing at them. Owls perched blinking on the henroosts. Foxes mingled with the hens. Monkey hung by his tail from a beam. At a door of the barn a long-eared donkey stood patiently waiting, his eyes closed and his head drooping as if he had reached the end of a long journey. The camels also waited in the barnyard.

Miss Hickory darted around to the cathole, but however she tugged at it she could not open it. At last she crept in and out of the maze of legs in the barnyard until she was just inside the barn door. She could go no farther. No one harmed her, but no one made a way. They all seemed to share a secret that she had been too stiff-minded to believe. So she waited there, and at midnight the Christmas star entered the barn. It shone straight down through the roof and made a line of gold that rested above Wild-Heifer's stall. There was suddenly a sound of rushing wings outside. Then the creatures, every one, kneeled down on the barn floor and bowed their heads.

"What is it?" Miss Hickory asked Squirrel. "I can't see."

Squirrel pushed her head hard, but her neck was too stiff for bowing. "I told you," he whispered. "Wild-Heifer's manger holds—" But the sound of his voice was drowned by such a pealing of the icicles that Miss Hickory lost the last of his words. The creatures arose. They had all, except Miss Hickory, seen the golden imprint in Wild-Heifer's manger.

The light of the Christmas star faded and the procession of strange creatures formed and started back toward Temple Mountain. The barn door closed and there was again only her same snowy world, but it was Christmas morning. Miss Hickory started home. She met Fawn, who was feeding alone through the snow of the Acre-Piece. In High-Mowing the hen-pheasants of the Ladies' Aid Society were setting themselves beneath their bed quilt. Not a cock-pheasant was in sight. When she reached Squirrel's hole she peeped in. He was alone, busily cracking the nuts that he should have been saving. Winter had still far to go.

"If I hadn't seen it, if I hadn't been there, I should say that I dreamed it," she thought. Then, all at once, Miss Hickory felt something was really wrong with her. "I should have paid heed to Squirrel," she thought. "'I might have seen inside the manger in the barn, but I was hardheaded."

CAROLYN SHERWIN BAILEY

Dr. Watts's Cradle Hymn

Hush my dear, lie still and slumber,
    holy angels guard thy bed,
Heavenly blessings without number,
    gently falling on thy head.

146

How much better thou'rt attended
   than the Son of God could be,
When from heaven he descended,
   and became a child like thee.

Soft and easy is thy cradle,
   coarse and hard thy Saviour lay,
When his birth-place was a stable,
   and his softest bed was hay.

See the kinder shepherds round him,
   telling wonders from the sky;
There they sought him, there they found him,
   with his Virgin Mother by.

See the lovely Babe a-dressing;
   lovely infant how he smil'd!
When he wept, the Mother's blessing
   sooth'd and hush'd the holy child.

The New England Primer

In the Great Walled Country

AWAY AT THE NORTHERN end of the world is a land full of children, called The Great Walled Country. All around the country is a great wall, hundreds of feet thick and hundreds of feet high. It is made of ice and never melts; and for this reason more people have not discovered the place.

Nobody who lives there ever grows up. The king and queen, the princes and courtiers play a great deal with dolls and tin soldiers, and every night at seven o'clock have a bowl of bread and milk and go to bed. But they make excellent rulers, and the other children are well pleased with the government.

Grandfather Christmas lives just on the north side of the country, so his house leans against the great wall. Grandfather Christmas is his name in The Great Walled Country; no doubt we should call him Santa Claus here. Best of all the children in the world, he loves the children behind the great wall of ice.

One very pleasant thing about having Grandfather Christmas for a neighbor is that in The Great Walled Country they never have to buy Christmas presents. Every year, on the day before Christmas, Grandfather Christmas goes into the great forest of Christmas trees back of the palace of the king and fills the trees with candy and books and toys and all sorts of good things. When night comes, all the children wrap up snugly and go to the forest to gather gifts for their friends. Each one goes by himself so that none of his friends can see what he has gathered, and no one ever thinks of such a thing as taking presents for himself.

So Christmastime is a great holiday in that land.

But there was a time, many years ago, when the children in The Great Walled Country had a very strange Christmas. There came a visitor to the land, an old man, the first stranger for many years who had succeeded in getting over the wall. He looked so wise and was so much interested that the king invited him to the palace.

When this old man was told how they celebrated Christmas, he said to the king, "That is all very well, but I think that children who have Grandfather Christmas for a neighbor could find a better way. Why not go out together, and everyone get his own presents? Everyone would be better satisfied."

This seemed to the king a very wise saying, and he called his courtiers and counselors to hear it. They agreed they had been very foolish never to have thought of this simple way of getting their Christmas gifts. They said, "We will make a proclamation, and always after this follow the new plan."

The plan seemed as wise to the children of the country as it had to the king and the counselors. Everyone had at some time been a little disappointed with his Christmas gifts; now there would be no danger of that.

On Christmas Eve they always had a meeting at the palace, and sang carols until time for going to the forest. On this particular night it seemed to the king that the music was not so merry as usual and that when the children spoke to one another their eyes did not shine as gladly as in other years. But there was no good reason for this, since everyone was expecting a better time than usual.

There was only one person at the palace that night who was not pleased with the new proclamation. This was a little boy named Inge, who lived with his sister. Now his sister was a cripple and had to sit all day looking out of the window from her chair. He had always gone to the forest on Christmas Eve and returned with arms and pockets loaded with pretty things for his sister, which would keep her amused all the coming year.

But now, said Inge to himself, what would his sister do? After thinking about it a long time, he silently made up his mind not to obey the proclamation. He decided it would not be wrong if, instead of taking gifts for himself, he took them for his sister.

And now the chimes had struck ten. The children were making their way toward the forest in starlight that was so bright that it almost showed their shadows on the sparkling snow. As soon as they came to the edge of the forest, they separated, each going by himself.

Ten minutes later, if you had been in the forest, you might have seen the children standing in dismay with tears on their faces. As they looked eagerly about them to the low-bending branches of the evergreen trees, they saw nothing hanging from them that could not be seen every day in the year. High and low they searched, wandering farther into the forest than ever before; but still no presents appeared.

As the children went trooping out of the forest, after hours of weary searching, some of them came upon little Inge, who carried over his shoulder a bag full to overflowing. He cried, "'Are they not beautiful things? I think Grandfather Christmas was never so good to us before."

"What do you mean?" cried the children. "There are no presents in the forest."

"No presents!" said Inge. "I have my bag full of them." But he did not offer to show them, because he did not want the children to see that they were all for his little sister.

Then the children begged him to tell in what part of the forest he had found his presents, and he turned back and pointed to the place where he had been. "I left many more behind than I brought away," he said. "There they are! I can see some shining on the trees even from here."

But when the children followed his footprints in the snow to the place where he had been they still saw nothing on the trees, and thought that Inge must be dreaming. Perhaps he had filled his bag with cones from the evergreen trees.

On Christmas Day there was sadness all through The Great Walled Country. But those who came to the house of Inge and his sister saw plenty of books and dolls and beautiful toys piled about the little cripple's chair. When they asked where these things came from, they were told, "Why, from the Christmas-tree forest."

And they shook their heads, not knowing what it could mean.

The king held a council and appointed a committee to visit Grandfather Christmas and see what was the matter. The committee set out on their journey. They had very hard work to climb the great wall of ice between their country and the place where Grandfather Christmas lived, but at last they reached the top. And when they came to the other side of the wall, they were looking down into the top of his chimney. It was not hard to go down this chimney into his house, and when they reached the bottom of it they found themselves in the very room where Grandfather Christmas lay sound asleep.

It was hard to awaken him, for he always slept one hundred days after his Christmas work was over. But at last Grandfather Christmas sat up in bed rubbing his eys.

"Oh, sir!" cried the prince who was in charge of the committee, "we have come from the king of The Great Walled Country, to ask why you forgot us this Christmas and left no presents in the forest."

"No presents!" said Grandfather Christmas. "'The presents were there. You did not see them, that's all."

But the children told him that they had searched carefully, and in the whole forest there had not been found a Christmas gift.

"Indeed!" said Grandfather Christmas. "And did little Inge find none?"

Then the committee was silent, for they had heard of the gifts at Inge's house and did not know what to say.

"You had better go home," said Grandfather Christmas, "and let me finish my nap. The presents were there, but they were never intended for children who were looking only for themselves. I am not surprised that you could not see them. Remember that not everything that wise travelers tell you is wise." And he turned over and went to sleep again.

The committee returned silently to the Great Walled Country, and told the king what they had heard. When next December came, he made another proclamation, bidding everyone to seek gifts for others, in the old way, in the Christmas-tree forest. So that is what they had been doing ever since.

RAYMOND MACDONALD ALDEN

Christmas Carol

The earth has grown old with its burden of care,
  But at Christmas it always is young,
The heart of the jewel burns lustrous and fair,
And its soul full of music bursts forth on the air,
  When the song of the angels is sung.

It is coming, Old Earth, it is coming to-night!
  On the snowflakes which cover thy sod.
The feet of the Christ-child fall gentle and white,
And the voice of the Christ-child tells out with delight
  That mankind are Children of God.

On the sad and the lonely, the wretched and poor,
  The voice of the Christ-child shall fall;
And to every blind wanderer open the door
Of hope that he dared not to dream of before,
  With a sunshine of welcome for all.

The feet of the humblest may walk in the field
  Where the feet of the Holiest trod,
This, then, is the marvel to mortals revealed
When the silvery trumpets of Christmas have pealed,
  That mankind are the children of God.

PHILLIPS BROOKS

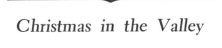

Christmas in the Valley

As DAVID WALKED over the snow carrying two buckets of milk for Mrs. Orville Byrd, he thought about the Christmas present for his grandmother. He milked two cows every night and morning for Mrs. Byrd and he made fifty cents a day for doing this. David gave his money to Grandma. Prices had gone up on everything, and with his hound dog Orphan to feed, it took more money for his grandmother and for him.

As he walked, the December snow crunched beneath his feet and the winter wind sang lonesome songs without words in the leafless apple-tree boughs over his head. He thought, At Christmas I want to make Grandma Beverley the happiest woman in the world. She has been the best person to me that I've ever known. I want to get her a wonderful present. But how am I going to get a present without any money? We need all the money we've got just to live.

David had been thinking about this present since November. Now there were seven more days to Christmas, and he had no wonderful present for Grandma. I can't get a dress for Grandma, he thought. I can't get her a water bucket—we have two. I can't get dishes. David didn't know where to get pretty dishes like those he had seen in Mrs. Byrd's dining room. He had been in her dining room twice. Once she invited him in out of a storm. Once she called him and told him what to do with the milk when she and Mr. Byrd were going away for the weekend.

155

When David took the milk to the cellar on this cold winter evening, Mrs. Byrd opened the kitchen door and said, "Come in, David, after you've finished with the milk. I want to see you before you leave."

David put the milk in the separator. And he almost raised a sweat in the warm cellar as he turned the separator by hand. Then he poured the cream in one can, the skimmed milk in another, as he had always done. He washed the separator and then he went in to see what Mrs. Byrd wanted.

"David, I was talking to Mr. Byrd last night and he wants you to cut a cord of stovewood for us," she said. "You've been a good worker for us. Best we've ever had to milk our cows and take care of the milk."

"When do you want me to chop the stovewood, Mrs. Byrd?" he asked, his face beaming. Here is my chance to make some money, he thought quickly.

"Not until after the Christmas holidays," she said.

"Oh, all right, Mrs. Byrd," he said slowly. David was so disappointed he could hardly speak.

Mrs. Byrd was sitting before her kitchen fireplace. She had a piece of cloth on her lap. It was cloth that looked familiar to David. As she talked to him, she never stopped raveling threads. She was working on a big cloth, going round and round the square, raveling threads and tying fringes. On a little round table near her there was a small pile of little square pieces of old wine-bottles design, which was in the big square she was working on.

"Mrs. Byrd, I don't want to ask you a silly question," David said. "But I've seen that cloth some place!"

"You certainly have," she said, laughing. "You saw it down at the barn. It's a feed sack."

"What are are you making?" he asked.

"A tablecloth and napkins," she replied. "Just two feed sacks of the same color and I'll have a tablecloth and nine napkins."

"Oh, they're beautiful," David said so quickly that Mrs. Byrd stopped her work and looked up at him. "I would like to know how to make them."

"Pull up a chair and I'll show you," she said. She was pleased that David was interested.

"See, David, the sack is sewed up," she said, picking up a sack at her feet. "First you shake the loose feed from it."

"Wouldn't you wash it first?" David asked.

"If you do it won't fringe as easily. Turn it wrong side out," she said, turning the sack. "Start unraveling it at this corner." She unraveled the sack to show him.

"That's simple," David said. "I can do that."

"Sure you can," she smiled. David watched her closely.

"The sack has two selvage sides, see," she said. "Tear them off so the sack will ravel."

Then she showed him how to ravel the sacks and tie the fringes. She showed him how to take one sack, divide it into three equal parts, then how to take each one of these pieces and divided it into three equal parts.

"Will you sell me two of the empty sacks down at the barn?" David asked. There was a new light in David's eyes.

"Go hunt yourself two of the prettiest sacks down there," she answered. "I'll give them to you."

"Thank you, Mrs. Byrd," David said, leaving her kitchen in a hurry.

David knew that he and his grandmother didn't have any sacks at their house. He never had seen feed-sack tablecloths and napkins before. But he knew that if Mrs. Byrd made them, they were all right. She had the prettiest house in the Valley. She had the house people came to see.

David went to the big wooden box in the barn where the empty feed sacks had been thrown. And he found two sacks of the prettiest color he'd ever seen. They were the autumn oak-leaf design. He knew these were the right sacks, for his Grandma Beverley had always liked the October days when the leaves turned and the lazy autumn winds swirled them down.

That night after Grandma Beverley had gone to bed, David sat up and worked on his tablecloth and napkins. This was a new kind of work for David. He was very slow at first and he found the tying of the threads very difficult. But he kept on working and the longer he worked, the easier his work became. He got the tablecloth finished in three nights. On the fourth and fifth nights he sat up after his Grandma Beverley had gone to bed and made six of his napkins. He worked each night until midnight. Grandma Beverley was fast asleep and never knew when David went to bed. On the sixth night, David finished the last three napkins.

"Talk about something pretty," he said to himself. Then he took them in the kitchen and spread them over the oilcloth on the table. "Grandma will surely love these."

The next morning when David went to milk for Mrs. Byrd, he took his tablecloth and napkins. After he'd milked and separated the milk, he showed them to Mrs. Byrd.

"David, this is the prettiest tablecloth and napkins I've ever seen," she said. "You have good taste. You selected sacks I had overlooked. How perfectly beautiful!"

When David told her what he was going to do with them, tears came to Mrs. Byrd's eyes. "You won't have to wash and iron them after she goes to bed," Mrs. Byrd told him. "I'll wash and iron them for you. I'll put them in a nice box and wrap them, too."

That evening after David milked for Mrs. Byrd, he knocked on the door. Mrs. Byrd gave him the box, wrapped in Christmas trimmings. "Here's a little present for you, David," she said. "I have a little pig out there in a box on the back porch. It is a runt pig. Our sow had fifteen. One more than she could feed."

"Oh, thank you, Mrs. Byrd," David said. "Your fixing Grandma's present was enough for me. But you couldn't have given me a nicer Christmas present than a pig. Grandma won't have to buy us a pig next year."

David took the present for Grandma and the box with the pig. When he got home he put the pig in the crib. Then he slipped up to his room while his grandmother was in the kitchen. David was as happy as he had ever been in his life.

Christmas Eve was as cold as they'd ever had in the Valley. The snow was a foot deep. And the wind had drifted small white ridges of snow against the fences.

"We are too poor to have much of a Christmas, David," Grandma Beverley said with a smile on her face. "This will be a cold Christmas night, too."

"But I have a present from Mrs. Byrd to show you in the morning," David said. "I'll mend the fire so we'll have fire all night. This is the coldest night we have ever had, Grandma."

When his grandmother went to bed, David pretended he was going to bed, too. He went upstairs to his room and waited until he was sure she was asleep. Then he slipped into her room and found her shoes under the side of her bed. He put the box on top of her shoes.

The next morning David was up and had rekindled the fire from the living embers. The bluster of mad winds roared around their house and banged their gates. It moaned through the branches of the leafless sassafras that stood beside the well in their back yard. It was Christmas at their house, all right. One of David's socks was filled with two bananas, an orange, and striped candy. And the other sock was filled with mixed nuts. These were the things David looked forward to getting since he had known there was a Christmas.

After David made a fire in the kitchen stove, he went out to feed the chickens and cow. This was Christmas morning and he was feeding early. He wanted to give his grandmother time to be up and dressed.

When David came in from feeding, his face was numbed by the raw winter wind. He carried a box into the house. Grandma Beverley was up and dressed and sitting before the fire. She had the table-cloth and napkins on her lap.

"David, look," Grandma Beverley said softly, tears coming from her eyes and rolling down her wrinkled face. "I wonder where this nice tablecloth and napkins came from."

"Made them from feed sacks," David said.

"The prettiest things I ever saw in my life," she said. "Who in the world would have ever thought of making a tablecloth and nap-kins out of feed sacks!" Grandma Beverley fondled the tablecloth and napkins like a little girl fondles her dolls on Christmas morning.

"David, what have you got in that box?" his grandmother asked. "It couldn't be a pig I hear grunting?"

"That's what it is, Grandma," he said proudly. "It's a Christmas present from Mr. and Mrs. Byrd. Their sow had more than she could feed. So she gave me the runt pig for Christmas!"

"Oh, that's wonderful, David," she said, looking down in the box at the little white pig. "Runt pigs make the finest hogs. We'll feed him after you look at your presents. Go back there and look on the dresser."

"Oh, Grandma," David shouted, setting his box with the pig on the floor. "Not this watch, Grandma?"

"Yes, it was your Grandfather Beverley's," she said. "I know he'd want you to have his gold watch."

David fondled the watch tenderly. Then he picked up a new pair of pants.

"Long dress pants for Sunday, David," his grandmother said. David was too stunned to speak. He was so overjoyed that tears came into his eyes.

"I'm so proud to have a son like you," she said. "I'm the proudest I've ever been in my life. You have brought me joy and happiness I have never known before."

Then Grandma Beverley got up and walked over to David. "Bend down," she said, "so I can hug and kiss you. You're taller than I am now. You're the beatinest boy that ever grew up in the Valley."

There was a new light in Grandma Beverley's eyes, and there must have been in David's, too, as they looked at each other on this white Christmas morning.

JESSE STUART

Lo, in the Silent Night

Lo, in the silent night a child to God is born,
And all is brought again that ere was lost or lorn.
Could but thy soul, O man, become a silent night,
God would be born in thee, and set all things aright.

Fifteenth Century Poem

162

A Tale of the Epiphany

THE CHRISTMAS BELLS had but lately ceased to ring out the message of peace and good will to all the world, and now the Feast of the Epiphany was drawing near. All around the city there hung an expectant air of holiday-making, and everyone was preparing for the great festa. The street boys made enough noise on their long glass trumpets to drive peaceful people mad, but the good-natured folk only clapped their hands over their ears and thanked the saints that such noise came but once a year.

There was scarcely a family, however poor, who would not have a fowl to cook for the coming festa, so trade was brisk.

Amidst all the noise of bargaining and blare of glass trumpets, a poor woman made her way through the crowded streets. Her thin old shawl was tightly wound round her shoulders, and in its folds was wrapped a little bundle the shape of a baby. Another child, three or four years old, clattered over the stone pavement at her side clutching a fold of the mother's gown. Behind came the tap, tap of wooden crutches as a bigger girl who was lame tried to keep up.

The woman looked wistfully at the array of fowls, and one of the sellers cried, "*Ecco,* this is the very thing thou seekest—so fat and tender." But the woman shook her head and hurried on.

163

"Mother," said Brigida, the lame girl, "shall we have no festa to-morrow?"

"Who can tell?" said the mother cheerfully. "Perhaps we may earn money today. If the master can but pay us, we may keep the festa with the best of them. A good boiled fowl and plenty of polenta, a gay new dress for the old doll thou lovest so well, a toy for little Maria here, and good milk for little Beppino. Who knows, we too may keep the festa!"

The faces of the two children brightened as she talked, and Maria's little legs, which had begun to drag wearily along, stepped out bravely once more.

"See, here we are," said the mother, stopping before a big, gloomy looking entrance and preparing to climb the steps which led up and up to the top story.

"Who comes there?" sounded a warning voice from above. "A friend," answered the woman and climbed steadily on, giving a helping hand to the tired child at her side.

At last they all reached the topmost flight, and there a door stood open, and a tall, stern-faced old man looked keenly out on the little family toiling up the last few steps.

"Ah!" he said, "so thou hast brought my model. Come in; the daylight fades all too soon these bitter days, and I would finish my work today if it be possible."

He let them into a great, bare attic, and bade the woman sit upon the old chair which he pulled forward. The children pressed close to their mother and looked about with round, surprised eyes. What a strange place this was! No table, no bed, nothing but piles of pictures standing with their faces against the walls, and in the center of the room on a curious wooden stand a great uncovered picture glowing with such wonderful color that it seemed almost to shine in the dull, dim room. The light from the sloping window fell full upon this picture, and as they looked the children forgot their shyness and fear of the stern-faced man and pressed forward to look at it.

It was a picture of the very festa they were preparing to keep next day, the feast of the Blessed Epiphany when the Three Kings brought gifts to the Christ child. There was the rough, rude stable, with the dim outline of cattle in the background; at one side an empty manger; and in the center where some straw had been heaped together, the Holy Mother with her Baby in her arms. Such a sweet young mother, as she gazed down with tender happiness upon the Child on her knee. Before them, on the rough stones of the stable floor, knelt the three kings, their heads bent in adoration, their costly robes of crimson, purple, and gold standing out in contrast to the dark stable and the simply clad mother. It was a wonderful picture, but disappointing too, for the best part was still unfinished, and only a blank showed where the face of the Gesu Bambino was still to be painted.

The old painter himself stood with the children looking at the picture and sighed. Day after day, month after month, he had worked at this picture, which he felt sure would at last bring him fame and honor. Faithfully and well he had worked, and each part was as beautiful as he could make it; only one thing was beyond his power. Toil as he might he could not paint the face of the Child as he wished it to be. Over and over again had he tried; he had sought models far and near, but it always ended in failure, and he painted it out each time in fresh despair.

But here was a new chance, a little model his quick eye had noted in yesterday's search. He bade the children stand back as he caught up his brushes, preparing to work. Then he turned impatiently to the woman. "Unwrap thy shawl and hold the baby so I can see his face," he ordered.

"He is asleep," she said, "and has a cough." But seeing the painter's angry, impatient look, she roused the child and arranged its blue pinafore and gently stroked its little, dark, downy head.

Beppino did not approve. He liked the soft shawl around him and wanted to sleep. So his nose began to wrinkle and his mouth to open wider, and a long-drawn wail come sobbing forth. Then followed coughing and more cries till the painter dashed down his brush and clapped his hands over his ears.

"Away with thee!" he cried; "as well bring a screaming parroquet for a model."

The angry voice stopped Beppino's cries for a moment, and he gazed across, his brown eyes full of tears, his lips quivering ready to start afresh. The woman spoke soothing words and Maria played bo-peep to make him laugh. But it was no use. The sobs broke out again louder.

"Take him away," said the painter, "it is but waste of time." He looked gloomily on as the woman wrapped Beppino in her shawl once more and took Maria's hand. Very wearily she walked toward the door, followed by the tap, tap of Brigida's crutches.

For one moment she looked around. Could she ask for just a little help? She had never begged of anyone before, but tomorrow was the festa and there was nothing for the children to eat. Some weeks ago little Beppino's mother had died, leaving him alone, and he had had his share of love and daily bread with her own two little ones. But an extra mouth, however small, was difficult to fill, and today she did not know where to turn for help.

She looked wistfully at the tall figure standing there. She tried to speak, but the words would not come. A dark frown had gathered

on the painter's forehead, and he turned impatiently from her beseeching look and stood before his picture.

With a sob the woman went down the long flight of stone steps.
It was no use looking at the fowls now or dreaming of gay presents.
Brigida saw the tears on her mother's cheeks as they silently trudged
homewards. "Thou art not angry with the little one, mammina?"
she asked. "It is not easy to sit and smile when one is cold and
sleepy."

The woman shook her head and tried to smile. "Poor lamb, it is no
fault of his; but there will be no festa for us tomorrow."

Maria opened her mouth and gave out one loud wail. No good
food, no sweet cake, no toy; it was more than she could bear.

"Hush now," cried Brigida, bending to kiss the miserable little
face. "I promise thee thou shalt have a beautiful present all thy
own," and she gave a mysterious nod and smile, which stopped
Maria's tears like magic.

Meanwhile in the attic the painter stood motionless before his picture and then sank in his chair in despair. All his hopes had been set on this picture, his greatest and best. He knew the work was good, but he began to fear it was beyond his power to finish. He saw nothing but the blank where the Christ-child's face should be, the center and heart of the whole picture, until at last he covered his eyes to shut out the sight of his bitter failure and disappointment.

Only a few minutes seemed to have passed when he looked up again with a start. A light seemed to shine from the unfinished picture, and he felt rather than saw that the picture was unfinished no longer. The light which dazzled his eyes was the halo of glory shining round the Christ-child's face—that face painted as even in his fairest dreams he had not pictured it. There was something so divine in the beauty of the little face that it seemed to make the attic a holy place, and the painter fell upon his knees, his eyes almost blinded by the glory.

But was it only a picture? He looked around. Where was he, and who were those kneeling figures beside him? This was not his attic but a stable, and instead of the kings in costly robes, the space before the gentle Mother and her Holy Child was filled with many figures crowding around, some richly dressed, some in rags, old and young, but each bearing some gift to offer to the Infant King.

Strange gifts were some; surely the Christ-child would refuse such mean offerings. But no, His hand was stretched out to receive even the commonest, and, strange to say, some gifts that seemed the poorest, at His touch were changed to such beauty that they shone like pure gold. Others that looked fit offerings for a king, piles of gold and gems, turned to lead and worthless pebbles.

A voice whispered in the painter's ear, "It is love that makes an offering really precious. Wherever Self creeps in, it spoils the most costly gift."

Now the painter felt he was being pressed forward, nearer and nearer. Then the thought flashed upon him that he had no offering to make; he alone of all the throng was kneeling there with empty hands. He searched his past life to find if he had any excuse to offer the Child King. He saw Self at every turn. He had lived for Self, and now his hands were empty.

Sobs shook his shoulders when he thought that soon the Blessed Child would smile on him, would stretch out His hand toward him, and he would have nothing to place there, no offering to make this glad Epiphany morning. Everyone except he had something. Even the little lame girl in tattered clothes kneeling beside him, clasped in her arms an old wooden doll. He alone had nothing, and every moment he was drawing nearer.

Only three people were in front of him now—a man grasping a handful of gold, a poor woman carrying a tiny baby, and the little lame girl with her battered doll. The man walked confidently up, but lo! when the gold touched the outstretched hand, it lost its shining and was changed to dull lead. Strangely enough, the man did not seem to notice, for he never glanced upward and did not see the grieved look on the Christ-child's face.

Timidly the poor woman came nearer. Kneeling down she whispered she had nothing to give because the baby she held was a motherless waif and her offering had been spent in giving it food and shelter. Ah! The painter saw in the Christ-child's hand a golden scroll on which was written in shining characters, "Inasmuch as ye have done it unto one of the least of these My brethren, ye have done it unto Me."

The little lame child came next. She gazed up with perfect trust as she held out the old wooden doll. It had been her one treasured possession, and was very hard to part with, but the little sister had nothing for the festa and had so longed for a real present. It was only an old doll, but it shone as brightly as the costliest gifts.

Then the painter knew it was his turn. Kneeling humbly he covered his face with his hands while he spoke. "I am but a poor man, too poor, Lord, to offer Thee anything, nor have I ever had the opportunity of doing anything for Thee."

But the Child bade him look. There before him was his old attic again, and a poor woman holding a baby, and two children clinging to her skirts. He saw the beseeching look in her eyes as she turned to go, and heard her half-choked sob as the door closed behind her. He started forward to stop her, but the vision faded. The voice sounded sorrowfully in his ear, "Inasmuch as ye did it *not*."

The painter wakened with a start. He had been dreaming, but tears wet his cheeks and a new pain gnawed at his heart. He could scarcely see the dim outline of his picture as he groped for his hat and felt his way to the door. Down the stone steps he hastened and into the silent night, with but one thought in mind. The streets were very quiet, but ere long the bells would ring out their glad welcome to the joyous festa day and he must do his errand quickly.

Before long he reached the poor street he sought, climbed the steep stairs and stood before a closed door. Hastily he drew something round from his wallet, wrapped it in a piece of paper, and carefully pushed it under the door until the last scrap of paper disappeared. Then he turned to go with a look of happiness such as his face had not worn for years.

"Get thee up, Brigida, dost not hear the bells?" cried the mother.

"We must not be late in going to church to greet the Gesù Bambino."

"Truly, mother," answered Brigida, rubbing her eyes, "the night seemed short, and I dreamed I had been to greet Him already." Her face shone with such a happy smile that her mother stooped to kiss her.

A shriek of joy from the other little bed made them start. Then they laughed with joy too. There sat Maria staring round-eyed at the old wooden doll which dangled from the end of the bed in front of her. "For me?" she shouted, stretching her arms toward it, as if it must be too good to be true.

"Yes, it is thy festa gift," said Brigida, with a wise little womanly shake of her head. "I am growing too old for playthings and this is for thy very own."

Even Beppino set up a feeble little crow of pleasure as he listened to Maria's shouts of delight, as she clasped the old doll in her arms. The poor mother too smiled at the sound, though her heart was heavy when she thought of the long day before her and the small piece of bread which was all she had to fill those hungry little mouths.

"Come, children," she cried, "let her hurry, or the bells will stop before we can reach the church."

She wrapped Beppino in her shawl, helped fastened Maria's frock, and then began to unlock the door.

"See, Mother," said Brigida, stooping and lifting a piece of paper, "someone pushed this under the door."

"Only a piece of dirty paper," said the mother. But as she opened it she cried, "Children, it is a piece of silver! It is money to buy all we need today." She stood and gazed at the silver piece, amazed.

"Mammina," shouted little Maria. "It is a gift from the Gesu Bambino for His festa, is it not so?"

"Now we shall have a fat fowl and sweet chestnuts, and Beppino will have the good white milk he loves," cried Brigida for joy.

But the mother did not seem to heed. There was an awed, thankful look on her face. "Hush, children, not so much noise. We must first go to thank the Blessed Child for His birthday gift."

The streets were already filled with hurrying people and the air was gay with the sound of bells, as the little family wended its way to the square and up to the steps to the front of the great church. The door stood open and the mother had only to push the leathern curtains aside to let the little ones pass in. First she pulled her handkerchief over her head and laid white squares on the two girls' heads.

Hand in hand they walked slowly up the great dim church to where light shone from the candles of a distant altar. There on the pavement they knelt in solemn reverence. Even the baby face of Maria looked awed as she folded her hands and tried to say her Latin prayer, which ended with her own words, "And I thank Thee, Little Lord Jesus, for this Thy birthday gift."

There was a stir in the world of Art. Men crowded to the convent chapel to see the new picture, about which everyone was talking.

"Really a wonderful piece of work," said the prior, "and to think we never knew until now how great a painter dwelt in our city!"

"Ah, we knew him well enough," said a brother artist standing near, "but never before has he painted like this. His work was always good, but it lacked life and soul."

"It would seem he has found his soul at last," said the prior as they all gazed reverently at the great Epiphany picture.

AMY STEEDMAN

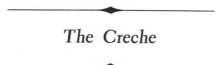

The Creche

WHO MUST BE THERE? The Child and His mother, without them there would be nothing at all. And there must be the Star overhead and the lambs in the straw at their feet, to remind the beholder that Jesus was born between heaven and earth, partaking of each. Old Joseph must be there to guard and love them, and the ox and the ass who shared the broken stable, and the three kings with the beautiful names bearing their gifts, as symbols of all the races of the earth.

The children admire the three kings with their rich robes and their golden crowns and their kind, happy faces. But they cannot look at them long. Nor can they look long at the lambs and the ox and the ass. Their eyes wander even from old Joseph with his white beard, to fasten on the Child in the lap of His young mother, and on the Star which shines down upon them so tenderly.

ELIZABETH COATSWORTH

173

Now Every Child

Now every Child that dwells on earth,
Stand up, stand up and sing!
The passing night has given birth
Unto the Children's King.
Sing sweet as the flute,
Sing clear as the horn,
Sing joy of the Children
Come Christmas the morn!
Little Christ Jesus
Our Brother is born.

ELEANOR FARJEON

To Make an Advent Wreath

AN ADVENT WREATH may be made of artificial green leaves that are non-inflammable, or of fresh evergreens which may be moistened occasionally during the four weeks of Advent. Make four spaces in the wreath large enough to hold nine-inch candles. In each space place a piece of clay as a base and press the candle firmly into it to hold it upright.

Or, you may use as a base an aluminum pie plate. Pour into it melted paraffin or plaster of paris about one inch deep. When this is partially hard, set into it at intervals around the edges, the four nine-inch candles. Check often to be sure the candles stand upright while the mixture hardens. Then cover the paraffin with a layer of sand and insert into it fresh evergreens. Moisten the sand frequently to keep the evergreens fresh.

A ring of styrofoam two inches thick can also be used as a base for the wreath. Cut holes in it for the candles.

You may decide to surprise your family or your club or group by making an Advent Wreath and planning what to do on the first Sunday in Advent. After that different people may share in the planning. Stories and verses from many different places and times, such as are in this book, add to the joyful preparations during Advent and to your Christmas happiness.

You will find suggestions for using your Advent Wreath and lighting the Advent Candles in the introduction to this book.

Index